SPACE POLICE:
ATTACK OF THE
MAMMARY CLANS

David Blake

www.david-blake.com

Edited and proofread by Lorraine Swoboda

Published in Great Britain, 2018

ISBN: 9781973564386

DEDICATION

For Akiko, Akira and Kai.

THE SPACE POLICE SERIES INCLUDES:

1. Attack of the Mammary Clans
2. The Final Fish Finger
3. The Toaster That Time Forgot

CONTENTS

ACKNOWLEDGMENTS

I'd like to thank my family for putting up with me and my rather odd sense of humour.

I'd also like to thank my editor and proofreader, Lorraine Swoboda, for making sure that what I write makes sense, sort of, and that all the words are in the right order.

CHAPTER ONE

DETECTIVE INSPECTOR Andrew Capstan was having a bad dream. It wasn't just your average bad dream, like when something slightly scary happens and you wake up. No: this was one of those nightmarish dreams where the same thing kept happening, over and over again, like when your grandmother keeps phoning you up to ask why her computer's not working, and it takes you over an hour to work out that she's been talking about the microwave.

And it felt like it had been going on and on to the point where Capstan was beginning to wonder if it was a dream at all, or if he'd somehow fallen down a giant wormhole and had ended up stranded in a parallel universe where a single day only lasted for a few minutes, so making life seem even more repetitive than it normally did.

Try as he might, he didn't seem able to wake himself up from it either, something he would have been delighted to do, especially during the middle part where he found himself doing something that made him want to be sick, each and every time he did it.

The dream always started the same way. He'd be standing next to his subordinate, Sergeant Dewbush, on a street corner in Bath during an unusually hot

British summer's day, keeping a certain female suspect's house under close observation. From behind them they'd hear the sound of an ice cream van approaching, and Sergeant Dewbush would ask, 'Would you like an ice cream, sir?'

That's when the dream would start to become disturbing, because Capstan would find himself replying, 'That would be very nice, thank you, Dewbush,' in a polite and highly appreciative manner, and without so much as a hint of sarcasm. He wouldn't normally answer a question put to him by his mentally challenged subordinate, not in quite such a respectful manner at any rate. It just wasn't something he would ever do.

Capstan would then observe his sergeant, instead of the house as he was supposed to, who'd flag down the approaching ice cream van by standing in front of it and holding out his formal police identification. He'd return about a minute later carrying two extra-large strawberry-flavoured Mr Whippy ice creams, but just as he'd hand one over to Capstan, the sergeant would drop it on the pavement, where it would land upside down on top of a large pile of dog poo.

Retrieving it from the poo, the sergeant would hand it to Capstan, saying, 'Sorry about that, sir,' to which Capstan would find himself replying, with genuine sincerity, 'That's all right Dewbush, I'm sure it wasn't your fault.'

And that's when the really disgusting thing would happen.

Despite every fibre of his being telling him not to, Capstan would give the dented, poo-covered ice cream a lengthy salacious lick, and would continue to do so until the whole thing had gone, and he was merrily munching his way through the cone.

When he'd finished, he'd return to watching the house as if nothing unusual had happened, until they'd hear the sound of another ice cream van, or possibly the same one, and at which point his sergeant would ask him, 'Would you like an ice cream, sir?'

As the whole horrific episode would start all over again, Capstan would find himself not only having to lick warm dog poo off the top of a half-melted Mr Whippy ice cream but, worst still, to continue to make the same appreciative remarks to his moronically inept sergeant each and every time he did so.

However, just before he was about to lick it for what must have been the four-millionth time, he finally managed to win the battle over his subconscious mind. And after a few moments spent stumbling his way through a dense deciduous forest that seemed to be made up of overgrown arrest reports and parking fine tickets, his eyelids flickered open and he found himself lying awake under the covers of a bed in a semi-darkened room, a rhythmic bleeping noise coming from somewhere over to his left, and a very familiar-looking person sitting beside him to his right, apparently playing a game on his phone. The bleeping sound to his left he assumed to be emanating from some sort of a heart rate monitoring machine; and the young man, who had tousled mousey-brown hair and a happy-go-lucky sort of a look to him, was none other than the person who'd featured so heavily in his dream.

'What time is it, Dewbush?' croaked Capstan, looking around the room for a glass of water, or something similar to help remove the bitter-sweet sensation of what tasted like strawberry and poo-flavoured ice cream from his mouth.

The young man jumped in his seat, and stared at him before glancing over both shoulders to see if he was addressing someone else in the room; but there was no-one else there.

'Didn't you hear me, Dewbush?' asked Capstan. He'd only been awake for about five seconds but was already feeling irritated.

'Er, the t-time?' asked the man, pushing himself up slowly from his chair.

'Yes, the time, Dewbush. You remember. That unit of measurement some of us use to know when to do things.'

'Of c-course,' answered the man; but instead of glancing at a wrist watch, or up to a clock on a wall, or even down at the phone he had in his hands, he began edging his way backwards, heading for the door.

'Surely it can't be that difficult a question, Dewbush, even by your standards?'

'Oh, um, no, but, well, um,' replied the man, as he continued to creep back towards the door.

'You don't even have to be exact.'

'Yes, but, I, er…'

'An approximate guess would do.'

'Well, I, er…'

'Tell you what, Dewbush, I'll make it easy for you. Is it the morning or the afternoon?'

'It's the, um, er…'

'The evening then?'

By then the young man had reached the door and, without taking his eyes off him, began fumbling with the knob.

'If the task of telling me the time is really too difficult for you, Dewbush, I don't suppose you could at least get me a glass of water?' asked Capstan.

But it was too late. The man had slipped out, and was already closing the door quietly behind him.

With a heavy sigh, Capstan rested his head back down on the pillow and stared up at the ceiling of what he assumed must be a private room in a hospital, and quite a modern one at that, judging by the decor. As he lay there he wondered why on earth his sergeant seemed not only unable to tell him the time, but to find the question unnerving to the point where he'd felt it necessary to flee the room instead of having to answer it.

That aside, he was feeling grateful for having woken up at all. The last thing he could remember, apart from having to repeatedly eat a dog poo-flavoured ice cream in some far off parallel universe, was being shot in the leg by a deranged bald fat psycho nut-job.

The bald fat psycho nut-job in question was Morose, who used to be the Chief Inspector of the Solent Police, but who'd since become the Serial Slasher of Southampton and the South Coast after being found guilty of killing numerous members of the local community in order to boost his quarterly police bonus. The incident of being shot in the leg had taken place on top of Ryde town hall in the middle of the Isle of Wight, where Capstan had managed to corner him, sort of.

With the memory of being shot came a sudden pain in his leg, and he instinctively reached down to touch it.

But - his leg. It wasn't there!

He could feel it, in his mind at least, he could even wiggle its toes. But where it should have been, lying next to the other one, it simply wasn't.

Surely it had to be, he thought, and lifted his head to look down the length of his body. However, his eyes only confirmed what his hand had discovered: that there was only one leg lying along the bottom half of the bed, and not the normal two he'd been expecting.

Having already managed to deal with the first stage of grief over the loss of his leg, that of denial, Capstan moved straight onto the second: anger. That psycho nut job Morose had shot him at virtually point blank range without so much as a care in the world, and if Capstan ever saw him again he'd be sure to make him suffer for it.

Then Capstan remembered that Morose's next shot had been meant for his head, and at that range it would have been unlikely that he'd have woken up at all. If it wasn't for the fact that the would-be killer had run out of bullets, it would have been far more likely that he'd currently be decomposing inside a coffin, or resting in an urn above the fireplace at his home after having been cremated, giving something else for his wife to dust around.

So Capstan transferred his anger towards the surgeon who'd cut the limb off without asking his permission first. That really was unforgiveable. It was his leg, after all, and although it had never worked particularly well after Rebecca of Bath had run over it with her Roman army several years earlier, at least he'd had the full complement. And as he'd had it since birth, he'd become rather attached to it, and doubted if there was much else in the world he could have been more attached to, apart from the other one, of course. Although, saying that, he also felt attached to his arms as well, not to mention his head, but he'd already established that without a head, or more importantly the brain inside it, it wouldn't matter all that much if he was missing a leg.

But he still felt the surgeon had had a professional obligation to ask him first, before deciding to take a hacksaw to it.

That led Capstan nicely into the third stage of grief, which psychologists refer to as bargaining, and he wondered, albeit momentarily, if he'd be able to get it back, maybe in exchange for something the hospital would need, like a pint of his blood, or perhaps one of his kidneys. But never having heard of anyone who'd had an amputated limb sewn back on before and been able to use it effectively afterwards, he was soon onto the fourth stage of grief, that of depression. This was a mental state his mind was familiar with, as he'd been depressed for about as long as he could remember. So he lay there for a few minutes feeling generally rather sorry for himself; and instead of thinking about his missing leg, he wondered where that idiot Dewbush had gone, and if he'd ever been able to tell the time, or if it was just something Capstan assumed he could do but had never asked him before, a bit like when Dewbush had been driving them both down the A3, chasing after Morose in a stolen YouGet delivery van, only to learn that he couldn't drive, or at least hadn't passed his test.

Remembering that he still hadn't had a drink, Capstan yelled out, 'COULD SOMEONE PLEASE GET ME A GLASS OF WATER, AND MAYBE SOMETHING THAT COULD TELL ME THE TIME, LIKE A CLOCK, FOR INSTANCE?'

CHAPTER TWO

ABOUT FIVE MINUTES later, the same door Dewbush had slipped quietly out of was flung open by someone who Capstan assumed to be a doctor, given that he was wearing a white coat over a shirt and tie, who strode in making a beeline for the end of Capstan's bed with Dewbush following after.

'And how's our patient doing?' he asked, in a loud operatic voice that somehow managed to express both authority and empathy in equal measure. And he continued to stand there, staring down at Capstan, with a clear expectation of some sort of a verbal response.

As Capstan observed Dewbush re-take his position beside his bed, he replied, 'I'm OK, I suppose, but I am a little thirsty.'

'That's quite normal.'

'And I wouldn't mind knowing what the time is, just out of interest?'

'Yes, well… I think we'd better start with the water and leave the discussion about the time until later.'

The doctor glanced over at Dewbush. 'Would you be so kind as to get Mr Capstan here a glass of water, please?'

'Yes, Doctor,' replied the man, before looking

down at Capstan and asking, 'Big, bigger, biggest or well-big?'

'I'm sorry?' said Capstan.

'What size glass of water would you like?' asked the man Capstan had always known as Dewbush. 'Big, bigger, biggest or well-big?'

By now Capstan's naturally suspicious nature was most definitely aroused. There was something distinctly odd about this entire scenario, the most obvious being that Dewbush was failing to include the word "sir" at the end of each sentence, something he'd never known him to do before, and which was in clear violation of the Police Code of Conduct. After all, Capstan was a detective inspector, whilst Dewbush was nothing more than a lowly sergeant.

There was also the peculiar terminology he'd used for the drink size options. Capstan was hardly a man who made a habit of keeping up with the latest trends, but even he would have known if everyone had started going around saying "big, bigger, biggest or well-big", instead of "small, medium, large or extra-large".

But for now Capstan decided to keep his suspicions to himself, and played along by answering, 'I'll have a big one, thank you, Dewbush.'

The doctor retrieved what looked like an iPhone from his white coat's top pocket, and began to study the screen. Capstan's eyes followed Dewbush as he made his way over to some sort of a large microwave, built in to the far right hand side wall. There he pressed a single red button on its front, leaned in towards it, and said, 'One big glass of water please.'

After a momentary pause, the machine replied, '*Hello, Peter Simon Dewbush. Good to see you again! I'll just get that for you,*' in a warm soft female voice with a distinctly American accent.

As Dewbush stuffed his hands into the trouser pockets of what Capstan now realised was a remarkably shiny, almost metallic-looking suit, the microwave piped up again. '*And would you like fries with that?*'

Dewbush turned around to look over at Capstan. 'Would you like fries with your glass of water?' he asked.

Capstan found himself unable to reply. His mind was just far too busy trying to work out how it was possible for the microwave to know Dewbush by name, how it could possibly provide him with the choice of having either a glass of water or fries, or indeed how it was able to talk to him in the first place.

With no response forthcoming, Dewbush shrugged, and turned back to the talking microwave. Leaning in towards it again, he replied, 'I think we'll just have the big glass of water, thank you.'

'*How about a cheeseburger instead of the fries?*' offered the microwave.

'No. Just the water, thank you,' said Dewbush.

'*Perhaps you'd prefer a milkshake, to go with your big glass of water?*'

'Again, just the water,' repeated Dewbush.

'*Are you sure I can't change your mind?*' asked the microwave. '*After all, we do have the thickest, creamiest milkshakes this side of the Andromeda Galaxy, and it's on special offer today at only $125, if purchased at the same time as our Super Deluxe Well-Big Cheeseburger and Fries Combo.*'

'Just the big glass of water will be fine, thank you,' said Dewbush, once again.

'*Are you absolutely sure I can't convince you to upgrade your order to include a Super Deluxe Well-Big Cheeseburger and Fries Combo to go with your big glass of water?*' asked the microwave.

'No, thank you.'

'*Knowing that you'd be getting a well-big milkshake for only an additional $125?*'

'Again, no!' repeated Dewbush, raising his voice a little, but considering the intense consumer pressure he seemed to be under, Capstan thought he was doing a remarkable job of remaining calm.

'*Does that mean you are sure or that you are not sure?*'

'I am definitely sure that I only want a glass of water!' stated Dewbush.

'*And there's absolutely nothing I could offer you that would help to change your mind?*'

'No, nothing!'

'*OK, no problem. And what size glass of water would you*

15

like; big, bigger, biggest or well-big?

Capstan heard Dewbush let out a heavy sigh. 'Didn't I already tell you that?'

'I'm sorry, you may well have done,' said the microwave. *'Hold on, let me replay our conversation to you.'*

'NO, PLEASE!' said Dewbush, sounding quite desperate. But almost immediately he seemed able to regain his remarkably calm composure to say, 'I asked for a big one, thank you.'

'And how many would you like? Please say "one" for one, "two" for two, "three" for three, "four" for four, "five" for five, "six" for six, "seven" for—'

'ONE!' stated Dewbush, almost shouting.

'One big glass of water coming right up!' announced the microwave, after which a little light came on inside it, and the machine began to make a whirring sort of a noise that sounded very much like a more traditional, non-talking one.

A few moments later it emitted a loud *"ping"* before announcing, *'That will be $250 please!'*

Capstan stared as Dewbush held his watch up to the machine which bleeped again, and the microwave said, *'Thank you for shopping with YouGet, Peter Simon Dewbush. Your order is now ready for collection.'*

Opening the door of what seemed to be an extraordinary new YouGet hole-in-the-wall automated shopping facility, Dewbush removed that which had appeared inside, closed the door, and turned to carry what was not so much a big glass of water, but more of a tiny, miniature-sized one, over to Capstan.

'One big glass of water!' announced Dewbush, with a look of triumphant relief as he handed it to Capstan.

Although Capstan would have loved to ask Dewbush a number of questions relating primarily to the discussion he'd just witnessed him have with a microwave, along with why something described as being a big glass of water was no bigger than a vodka shot, or why he'd paid for it in dollars instead of pounds, or how such a tiny glass of water could ever sell for a quite staggering $250, when you could pick up a five-litre bottle of the stuff from your local Safebusy's for only £1.95, at that precise moment all he could think of to say was, 'Thank you, Dewbush,' as he sat himself up in his bed to sniff at the so-called water, just in case it wasn't, and instead was something that could more realistically be sold for such an exorbitant price, like Tiger Shark Wee, or Rhino Horn Milk. But as it both looked and smelt like normal water, or at least it didn't smell of wee and didn't look like milk, Capstan drank it straight down, and was about to ask for another when he remembered what that would entail for this man who was now staring at him, who he'd always known as Dewbush. He certainly looked like Dewbush, but the Dewbush he'd known would have struggled to open a tin of cat food, let alone conduct intense negotiations over the purchase of a glass of water with a talking microwave.

Then Capstan realised that while he'd been staring at Dewbush, and watching his peculiar interactions with the microwave, the doctor seemed to have been using his iPhone to conduct an external examination of him; either that or he'd been taking a series of pictures of the entire length of his body and was therefore some sort of a pervert who had a thing for middle-aged police inspectors lying in bed who'd just woken up to discover that one of their legs was missing. And that reminded him, and he turned to stare directly at the doctor to ask, 'I don't suppose you know anything about what happened to my leg, by any chance?'

'Huh?' replied the doctor, looking up from his iPhone thing.

'My leg?' repeated Capstan. 'I don't suppose you know what happened to it?'

'How do you mean?'

'Like where it's gone, for example?'

With a confused look, the doctor stared down at Capstan's leg, or at least the shape of it underneath the blanket, and said, 'I think it's still there, isn't it?' before leaning over to give it a prod with his index finger.

'I meant the other one?'

'The other one?' repeated the doctor.

'Yes, you know. They normally come in pairs,' and

18

noticing the doctor just happened to have two of his own, he stared at them, saying, 'A bit like yours.'

'I see,' said the doctor, following his gaze before standing up straight to re-examine his iPhone thing.

'So, you had two before, did you?' he asked a moment later as he gave his screen a few swipes with his finger, possibly trying to find a medical note about it somewhere.

'No. I had three, but one fell off during puberty.'

Without raising his head from the screen, the doctor slowly swivelled his eyes around to stare at him.

Remembering that he was talking to a doctor, and therefore someone who'd be unlikely to understand the basic concept of sarcasm, Capstan thought it best to answer the question again, but in a slightly less facetious manner.

'Yes, I had two before. Now, if you could enlighten me as to the whereabouts of the one that doesn't seem to be there any more, I'd be eternally grateful.'

There was a lengthy pause, during which the doctor didn't move, but just continued to stare at Capstan, as if lost in thought. He suddenly put his iPhone back into his lab coat pocket and said, 'Mr Capstan, I think I have some news for you which you may find a little—distressing.'

'What, even more distressing than waking up to find that I've only got one leg?'

'Potentially, yes.'

19

Capstan couldn't think of anything that could be more distressing than slipping into an unconscious state with two legs, only to wake up with one, until he realised that there probably were a few other things he wouldn't like to have been parted with, and slowly brought his right hand up to slip it down inside the bed's covers, towards his groin.

Thankfully, they were still there; at least he could feel all the relevant bits with his hand, and made a mental note to make a visual confirmation the very next time he went to the toilet.

Feeling confident that there was nothing else he could think of that he could be parted from that would cause him distress, apart from maybe his wife leaving him, although that would probably have had the opposite effect, he drew his arm back out from under the covers and used it to fold together with the other, saying, 'Go on then, what is it?'

CHAPTER THREE

THE DOCTOR FOLDED his own arms, rubbed his chin with one of his hands and stared up at the ceiling before saying, 'Right then, where should I start?'

'How about at the beginning?' suggested Capstan.

'The beginning, yes, but the beginning of what?'

'The beginning of this thing you're about to tell me that you think's going to be even more distressing than discovering that I've only got one leg instead of the two I'd grown accustom to having.'

'I suppose that would be the best place; however, I don't actually know the beginning part.'

'Which parts do you know, then?'

'Just the middle and end bits, really.'

Capstan sighed. If it was going to take the doctor this long to decide where to begin telling whatever it was that he was going to tell him, he couldn't imagine how long it would take him to actually tell it.

'I appreciate that I'm not particularly busy at the moment,' said Capstan, 'being that I've only just woken up and that I still don't know what time it is, so I've no idea whether or not I have anything I should be getting on with, but I'm fairly sure you've at least got other patients to see. So I don't suppose there's any chance you could move things along a bit, otherwise I'll be needing another big glass of water.' Capstan glanced over at the man he still thought must be Dewbush, although he found himself becoming increasingly less convinced with every passing second.

'Yes, of course,' said the doctor. 'I suppose it all comes down to your question about time, really. What was that again?'

'I seem to remember simply asking what time it was,' replied Capstan. 'Why? Has my watch been stolen? Is that the distressing news you seem to be struggling to tell me?'

'Your watch—stolen? No, I don't think so, but time itself may have been.'

'What?' exclaimed Capstan, looking increasingly confused. 'Look, I don't mean to be rude, or anything, but who are you, exactly, and just what the hell is going on here?'

'I'm must apologise, Mr Capstan. I haven't even formally introduced myself yet. How inconsiderate of me. My name's Doctor Albright, and this here is Lieutenant Dewbush.'

'*Lieutenant* Dewbush?' asked Capstan, staring over again at the man who'd been a sergeant when he must have passed out on top of Ryde town hall in the middle of the Isle of Wight. He wasn't even aware that the rank of Lieutenant existed within the police, not the British police at any rate.

Lieutenant Dewbush, meanwhile, gave him a sort of half-wave and said, 'Hello!' before deciding to avoid the gaze of the man whom he'd been ordered to sit next to in preparation for him to wake up, and had been doing so for the last two days, during which time he'd had nothing better to do than to play Intergalactic Minecraft on his hand held touch-tech PalmPad device. And instead of returning the penetrating gaze of this rather intense-looking chap, he decided to examine his shoes for a while.

'Lieutenant Dewbush is the great-great-great-great-grandson of someone your data file suggested that you worked alongside, one Simon Peter Dewbush, who it said was a sergeant for what was then called the British Police Force. We're not sure exactly why, or anything, but at some point you were cryogenically frozen, possibly as part of an experiment, and you've been in a state of suspended animation ever since. So when we were told that a cleaner had forgotten to put the plug back in to your cryogenics machine after she'd finished hoovering the ship's deep space storage room, and that you'd begun to wake up, we thought it would help the process of assimilation into your new life if you had someone with you who has a direct, albeit remote, connection with your old life when you did.'

Capstan was now staring open-mouthed and unblinking at the doctor, and for one brief moment he actually believed what this man was telling him. But then he realised how utterly ridiculous that was, and that it was just an elaborate practical joke, probably thought up to help make him feel better about losing his leg. However, if Dewbush had gone to such extraordinary lengths to take his mind off his leg, probably with the help of Chief Inspector Chupples and the rest of the Solent Constabulary, he might as well go along with it for a while. So instead of spoiling the whole thing by laughing out loud and asking where the cameras were, with a serious tone instead he said, 'I see. Well, I can fully understand why you wanted to be so tactful in breaking this most alarming news to me.'

'So, in answer to your question, "What time is it?" it is in fact,' and he looked at his wrist watch, 'eleven fifty-two on the morning of Tuesday, 23rd May, 2459.'

'Right!' said Capstan. 'So, nearly lunchtime then?'

'I suppose it is,' said the doctor. 'I must say, Mr Capstan, I'm delighted to see how well you're taking all of this.'

'I'm probably still in shock,' said Capstan. 'So, I suppose we're all on a spaceship and that Earth was destroyed by a Global Thermal Nuclear War and is now a giant nature reserve inhabited only by mutated cockroaches and talking monkeys?'

'Not at all. Nuclear weapons were banned a very long time ago; but you are right about us being in space, though. You're currently in orbit around Earth on the UKA's Police Space Station 999.'

'Well, that's good to know. So, if I could have some lunch now, that would be great. I suddenly seem to be feeling rather hungry, especially now that I know that I've been asleep for around four hundred and fifty years. And then, afterwards, maybe you'd be kind enough to wheel me into a time machine and send me back to the year 2017, along with my leg?'

'I'm very sorry, Mr Capstan, but we're unable to do that. The use of time machines is strictly prohibited, so I'm afraid that you're just going to have to stick around with us here for a while.'

'Look, I think this has gone on for quite long enough, don't you?' asked Capstan, looking first at the doctor, and then over at Dewbush.

'I'm sorry, I'm not with you,' said the doctor.

'I understand why you're doing it,' Capstan continued, interchanging glances between the two of them. 'To help me to get over the loss of my leg. And I appreciate that, really I do. But making up some outlandish story that I've been asleep for four hundred and fifty years is just, well, it's just really stupid, and not even the slightest bit believable.'

'Ah, I see. You're doubting the reality of the situation,' said the doctor. 'I suppose that was to be expected. You're probably just at the first stage of grief over the loss of your former life on Earth. But don't worry. Before you know it you'll be moving on to the

25

second stage, anger, when you'll no doubt start shouting at all of us. Then will come the third stage, that of bargaining, at which point you'll probably offer to pay us large sums of money to break the law and send you back to the year 2017. After that you'll become depressed for a while, which is the fourth stage, but I'm sure that once you've had a chance to look around the place and have made some new friends, you'll soon reach the fifth and final stage of grief, that of acceptance, and the healing process will be complete.'

By the end of his little lecture about the human psychological process of dealing with loss, Capstan simply glared at the Doctor with a disgruntled look and his arms firmly locked together over his chest.

'Yes, well,' began the doctor, who didn't particularly wish to be around when Capstan moved into the second stage of grief and started shouting at him, which is what he looked like he was about to do, 'I do have a few more patients to see, as you so rightly suggested, so maybe if Dewbush here could get you some lunch, I'm sure you'll very soon start to feel better about the whole situation.'

CHAPTER FOUR

AFTER THE DOCTOR had gone, and Capstan was left with the man who allegedly wasn't Sergeant Simon Peter Dewbush after all, but his great-great-great-great-grandson, Peter Simon Dewbush, he said, 'So, what's on the menu?'

'Oh yes, of course,' said Dewbush, and made his way back to the microwave built in to the wall, behind which Capstan assumed must be someone hiding, like perhaps a girl from HR putting on an American accent. Once there he paused momentarily before pressing the red button again and with some trepidation, asked, 'Can I have the menu, please?'

'*Hello, Peter Simon Dewbush. Good to see you again. I'll just get that for you,*' said the microwave, in exactly the same way as it had done before.

While Dewbush waited, he turned around to notice that the man in the bed was still staring at him, and feeling a little self-conscious said, 'Won't be a moment,' before lifting himself up onto the balls of his feet and examining the ceiling.

He didn't have to wait long before the microwave came to the conclusion that more information was needed. '*And which menu would you like, Peter Simon Dewbush? Please say "Breakfast Menu" for the Breakfast*

Menu, "Brunch Menu" for the Brunch Menu, "Lunch Menu"
for the Lunch Menu, "Afternoon Tea Menu" for the Afternoon
Tea Menu, "Dinner Menu" for the Dinner Menu or "A Little
Something Before Bedtime Menu" for the A Little Something
Before Bedtime Menu.'

Dewbush leaned in and said, 'The *Lunch* Menu please.'

'*No problem, Peter Simon Dewbush. And would you like fries with that?*

'Just the menu, thank you,' said Dewbush.

'*Are you sure you wouldn't like to have fries with that?*

'NO! I really only want the Lunch Menu! Nothing else! Thank you very much!'

'*No problem, Peter Simon Dewbush. One Lunch Menu coming right up!*' and as before a little light came on inside, and after the microwave had whirred around for about ten seconds it pinged and said, '*That will be $37 please.*'

Once again Dewbush held his sleek black watch up to the machine, after which the microwave said, '*Thank you for shopping with YouGet, Peter Simon Dewbush. Your order is now ready for collection.*'

With a look of relief, Dewbush opened up the microwave's door and took out what appeared to be an ordinary-looking laminated menu. Turning back to the man in the bed again, he asked, 'Shall I read it out for you?'

'If you could, yes, please,' said Capstan.

Clearing his throat, Dewbush said, 'They've got Burger and Chips, Burger and Beans, Burger and Peas, Burger and Mash, Burger and Cheese, Burger and Bacon, Burger and Salad or just plain Burger,' before looking up expectantly at Capstan.

'I suppose that if I order a Burger and Salad,' began Capstan, 'the lady hiding behind the wall would say that they've only got Burger and Chips because they've run out of everything else, but the real reason would be because that's all you'd prepared to help facilitate this little charade of yours.'

But Dewbush didn't seem to have a clue what this man from the bygone age of the 21st Century was going on about, so he asked, 'Are you saying that you want the Burger and Salad?'

'To be honest, Dewbush, if that is your real name, I'm really not very hungry anymore.'

With a relieved look, probably because that meant that he wouldn't have to re-start negotiations with the microwave, Dewbush said, 'Well, if there's nothing more, I'll be off then,' and walked over towards the door.

'What do you mean, "If there's nothing more"?' asked Capstan, with a sudden feeling of insecurity brought on by the idea of being left alone.

'Er, well, I was only told to stay here until you woke up. And then I only continued to stay because Doctor Albright asked me to get you some lunch. So if there's nothing else you need, I'd better be getting back to my desk.'

'But—' began Capstan, unable to believe that that was it, and the end of this extraordinarily elaborate practical joke that wasn't even the slightest bit funny, even by practical joke standards, was this man, supposedly called Dewbush, simply walking out the door. So before he did, Capstan asked, 'What about my leg?'

'Oh, I shouldn't worry about that,' began Dewbush, just as his sleek black watch began emitting a neon blue light that faded in and out as it played a cheerful, upbeat sort of a tune. 'I'm sure they'll be able to sort something out for you,' he said, before lifting his wrist up to his mouth and saying, 'Lieutenant Dewbush here.'

'Lieutenant Dewbush, I have the Chief Inspector on the phone for you,' came a well-spoken woman's voice from his watch, the sound quality of which was so good, she could easily have been in the same room as them.

'The Chief Inspector?' asked Dewbush, with surprised alarm.

'That's correct.'

'You mean—Chief Inspector Chapwick, the Head of the UKA's Space Police?'

'Correct again.'

'And he wants to speak to *me?*

'I believe that is why he asked me to call you, yes, but I could be wrong. Shall I check for you?'

'Oh, er, no. I'm sure it's fine.'

'I don't mind asking him to confirm that it is you he wants to talk to, but I doubt if he'd appreciate having a lieutenant question his decision to phone you up.'

'No, no, that's fine. Please don't ask him! I'm happy to take the call.'

'Putting you through now,' said the lady, before another voice came over the line.

'Hello! Hello! Is anyone there?'

Hearing the Chief Inspector's voice, Dewbush stood to attention, and said, 'Chief Inspector Chapwick! It's an absolute honour, sir!'

'Lieutenant Bushdew, isn't it?'

'Oh, er, it's actually pronounced *Dewbush*, sir, but apart from that, yes, it's me, sir, at your service!'

'Good, good. Now I understand that you've been given the task of looking after that cryogenically frozen guy.'

'I have, sir, yes,' said Dewbush, looking over at the cryogenically frozen guy in question.

'And that he's been defrosted?'

'He has, sir, although I don't think he was supposed to be. Apparently a cleaner just forgot to plug his machine back in after she'd done a spot of hoovering.'

'Has he woken up yet?'

'He has, sir.'

31

'And…?'

'And what, sir?

'What's he like?'

'How do you mean, sir?'

'You know, what sort of condition is he in?'

'Well, he's only got one leg, if that's what you mean, sir.'

'No, no, no! I mean, what's his brain functionality like?'

'His brain functionality, sir?'

'Yes, you know. Has he retained the use of his synaptic nervous system, or did he wake up a complete vegetable like they normally do?'

'Oh, I see what you mean. Well, he's been sitting up in bed talking, so I'd say that he's in pretty good shape, all things considered, sir.'

'Excellent! Now, how long do you think it will be before I can meet him?'

'You want to meet him, sir?'

'Yes! And as soon as possible. Apparently, according to his file, he was one of the most highly decorated policeman of his day, and even had an OBE!'

'I see, sir. And that was good, was it, sir?'

'I've no idea, but I found it in his box of personal effects, and it looks impressive enough. Anyway, he sounds like just the sort of chap we could do with around here, so if he still has his full complement of marbles, then I'd be very keen to meet with the man.'

'Right, sir.'

'So…?'

'So…what sir?'

'So…how quickly do you think you'll be able to get him over here?'

'Oh, I'm not sure, sir. Hold on. Let me ask him for you.' Dewbush put a hand over his clever little phone watch thing, looked over at the man in the bed, and asked, 'I don't suppose there's any chance you'd like to meet the Chief Inspector, would you?'

Having been unable to do anything but listen in on the conversation, whether he wanted to or not, Capstan was becoming increasingly convinced that this wasn't some sort of elaborate wind-up after all, and that what the doctor had told him could well be the truth; that he had indeed been cryogenically frozen and it really was the year 2459. And finding himself to be almost excited by the prospect of actually being in the future, he thought he'd skip the second stage of grief over the loss of his former life and move straight into the third stage instead. On that thought he said, 'Tell you what, I'll meet him if I can have my leg back.'

Dewbush gave him an anxious sort of look and went back to his telephone conversation.

'Hello, sir. Are you still there?'

'Of course I'm still here!'

'He said he'd be happy to meet with you on the

condition that he could have his leg back, sir.'

'Have his leg back?'

'Yes, sir.'

'Who's taken his leg?'

'Nobody, sir. At least nobody here. I think they must have taken it off before, sir. Before he was cryogenically frozen.'

There was a pause from the other end and Dewbush was just about to ask if he was still there again when the Chief Inspector came back with, 'Very well…I suppose. I'll have one of our medi-bots sent down to fix him up with a new one. So, assuming they can find one that fits, shall we say…two o'clock?'

Looking again at the man in the bed, Dewbush repeated the Chief Inspector's question to him.

'If I can get a new leg by then, and something to wear, perhaps,' replied Capstan, 'then I should think two o'clock would be OK.'

Back into the watch, Dewbush said, 'He says two o'clock is fine, sir, but that he's going to need something to wear.'

'Doesn't he have any clothes?'

'Not that I can see, sir.'

'Very well. If you can sort something out for him through YouGet, that would be appreciated.'

'Yes, sir,' replied Dewbush, although not sounding particularly thrilled by the prospect of having to use the YouGet machine again. 'And is it all right if I pay for it through the Police Expense Account, sir? It's just that I've already had to buy him a glass of water, and a menu, sir, and I'm not sure that I'll have enough in my account if I have to buy him a whole new wardrobe as well, sir.'

'If you must. So, I'll see you both at two then, yes?'

'Yes, sir, and thank you, sir.'

Dewbush's watch phone's neon blue light went out, which apparently signified that the Chief Inspector had ended the call.

CHAPTER FIVE

A T PRECISELY two o'clock that afternoon, Capstan and the man he was beginning to think of as Dewbush, probably because he was, even though he wasn't, arrived at the desk of the Chief Inspector's PA.

As Dewbush waited for the lady sitting behind what seemed to be an invisible desk to get off the phone, so that he could tell her that they'd arrived for the meeting with the Chief Inspector, Capstan stared around at—well, just about everything really, and in very much the same way as he'd been doing since leaving his private care room and taking a lift up twenty five floors: as if he was a five year-old entering the Lego section of Toys"R"us for the very first time.

After the Chief Inspector had ended the call with Dewbush, Capstan had witnessed him exhibit exemplary conduct in the face of a fierce hostile sales and marketing campaign run against him by the YouGet machine, as he'd attempted to buy Capstan a new set of clothes. This would have been a challenging enough task under any circumstances, but one made all the harder by having to explain to the machine that the customer in question was a human male who only had one leg. And he'd very nearly completed the transaction when the medi-bot had arrived with Capstan's new appendage, something Dewbush had forgotten about. So he'd had to start all over again as the order was now for a human male with two legs.

The medi-bot itself, which looked like a remote-controlled female mannequin with short blue hair dressed up in a sexy nurses uniform, proved to be highly efficient, and within just a few minutes had attached what Capstan could only think of as a technological marvel: a false leg that looked like a real one and, once on, felt like one too. In fact, the only discernible differences were that its length could be adjusted, it was available in a choice of twelve colours, and it came with both a service manual and a log book.

At the end of the fitting he was also given a USB cable which the sexy medi-bot had advised him not to lose, but she'd failed to mention what it was for or where it was supposed to be inserted, or if she had then Capstan hadn't heard her, and with so much going on at the time he'd forgotten to ask.

With that USB cable in the bottom of the trouser pocket of his brand new, extraordinarily comfortable, and even more extraordinarily shiny new suit that was a sort of gun-metal colour, Capstan now stared open-mouthed at the invisible desk, trying to work out how on earth it could support the weight of the girl's elbows as she used what looked like a miniature blowtorch on her nails. When she finished with her call, she looked up at Dewbush, and flashing a set of teeth that were so incandescently bright that Capstan found himself having to squint to avoid damaging his retina, she asked, 'May I help you?'

Dewbush pulled out a pair of ultra-trendy looking sunglasses from his inside suit jacket pocket and put them on, saying, 'We're here to meet the Chief Inspector.'

The girl tilted her head at him, maintaining her immaculate smile before looking down at what should have been the top of the desk, but as there was nothing there, it looked more as if she was simply admiring her own legs, and for good reason. They were about as perfect as a pair of woman's legs could be, and Capstan couldn't help himself and joined her in staring at them, in very much the same way as he'd be doing at everything else. The girl swiped at the invisible desk's top a few times before looking back up to confirm who they were. 'Mr Capstan and Lieutenant Dewbush?'

'That's me!' answered Dewbush, 'I-I'm mean, I'm Lieutenant Dewbush and this is Mr Capstan.'

The unimaginably attractive girl swivelled her head around to stare at Capstan, but she did so in such a mechanical way that he momentarily wondered if she too was a robot, but a more advanced version of the sexy medi-bot girl he'd met earlier. She then gave him the full force of one of her smiles, forcing him to look away, and making him realise why Dewbush had made what had at the time seemed to be the rather peculiar decision to put sunglasses on.

'Right then,' she said, and stood up from her chair which again Capstan couldn't see, but assumed was a chair as she'd been sitting on it. She then walked around the matching invisible desk where she stopped, turned back to them again and said, 'If you could follow me please, gentlemen.' She then led them down a corridor which seemed to be exactly the same as every other corridor he'd so far been down in that both the floor and walls were a brilliant white colour, while the floor itself, although looking as if it was made up of highly polished tiles, underfoot felt more like rubber, reminding Capstan of the surface of the playground he'd once had to take his children to, when his wife hadn't been up to the task.

Arriving at the first door on the left, which looked very much like a normal door apart from the fact that it bore a blue neon sign that said "Chief Inspector Chapwick", she knocked.

From beyond the door they heard the muffled words, 'Come in!' and the PA stepped inside and announced, 'I have a Mr Capstan and a Lieutenant Dewbush to see you.'

'Thank you, Susan. Please show them in.'

CHAPTER SIX

A S THE CHIEF INSPECTOR'S PA stepped to one side, Capstan and Dewbush walked past her to find themselves in a large white room, decorated in much the same way as the corridor they'd just walked down, which seemed to be completely devoid of any furnishings. There wasn't even a window. All it had in it was a beige-coloured middle-aged man with mousey-brown hair, like Dewbush's, and wearing a very similar gun-metal suit, who seemed to be suspended half in the air in a sitting position, staring down at his legs, just like his PA had been doing.

When the suspended man heard the door close he looked up momentarily and, seeing two people standing on the floor in the middle of his office, said, 'Take a seat, won't you?' before returning to look as if he was examining his trousers.

Graciously, Dewbush invited Capstan to sit down first, which would have been fine, had he been able to see where he could do so. Not wanting to appear stupid, instead of accepting Capstan said, 'After you!'

With an ambivalent shrug, Dewbush stepped forward and placed his left hand beside a small luminescent red arrow which Capstan hadn't noticed before. He seemed to use that as a guide to allow him to sit straight down onto the chair that clearly must be there, even though it wasn't.

Following his lead, Capstan glanced over to the space next to where Dewbush was sitting to see that there were two similar arrows, the furthest one of which glowed red, and the closer one green. Stepping forward, he tentatively placed his left hand where the red arrow was pointing, just as Dewbush had done, and was amazed to feel something solid there that must have been some sort of an armrest. As he leaned in for a closer examination he could just about see the edges of it, but as soon as he stopped moving his head, it disappeared again. And after moving his head up and down a few more times he realised that it could only be seen if he kept doing so. But realising that he must have looked like some sort of giant pigeon that was attempting to make amorous advances towards an invisible chair, he glanced over to the other light, next to which he placed his right hand. And with due caution he then eased himself down so that he, too, was sitting, and in the most extraordinary chair he'd ever sat on in his entire life.

With his two guests now seated, Chief Inspector Chapwick looked up, first at Lieutenant Dewbush and then at Mr Capstan, who he recognised from having seen a four hundred and fifty year-old picture of him in his file, on a newspaper cutting from a publication called The Portsmouth Post. Observing his guest's

41

face for any signs of frostbite, none of which were obvious, he gave him a generous smile and asked, 'So, Mr Capstan, how's the 25ᵗʰ Century treating you so far?'

'It's alright, I suppose,' replied Capstan.

'It must have been a bit of a shock, to have been woken up after such a long time?'

'It does seem to be taking me a little while to get used to.'

'And I hear that Lieutenant Bushdew here is the great-great-great-great-grandson of your former police sergeant. Is that true?'

Capstan and Dewbush gave each other an embarrassed look, almost as if they were on some sort of gay TV dating show.

'So I've been told,' replied Capstan, moments later, and in the lieutenant's defence, added, 'although I believe his name is Dewbush, not Bushdew.'

Dewbush smiled at Capstan, which was the first time he had done. He was clearly grateful that Capstan had made the effort to correct the pronunciation of his surname.

'And did you know that you were going to be cryogenically frozen,' continued the Chief Inspector, 'or did they do it because you had some god-awful disease and thought it best to freeze you in the vague hope that someone might find a cure?'

'I must admit that I didn't know anything about

being cryogenically frozen. I was injured in the line of duty. The last thing I remember was being shot in the leg, after which I must have passed out. And then I woke up, here, about— what...' he instinctively looked down at his wristwatch before remembering that he didn't have one, and so decided to estimate how long it had been since he'd been awake, 'three hours ago.'

'Yes, and I was sorry to hear about your leg,' said the Chief Inspector. 'How are you getting on with the new one?'

'Rather well, actually!' replied Capstan, with a rare upbeat tone of voice, and he massaged the upper thigh section, still amazed at how real it felt.

'And what do you think of the view from here?' asked the Chief Inspector.

'The view?' questioned Capstan, unsure what he was referring to. 'I can't say I've seen the view yet.'

Turning to Dewbush, the Chief Inspector said, 'You haven't shown him the view?'

'I'm sorry, sir,' said Dewbush, 'but I haven't had the chance.'

'Well, don't worry. We can soon sort that out,' and with a quick swipe of the top of his invisible desk, the entire wall to their right began moving upwards as it slowly disappeared into the ceiling with nothing more than a gentle hum. And as it did, it began to reveal the most astonishing sight, which completely took

Capstan's breath away.

With his mouth hanging open he stood up from his invisible chair and wandered over towards the emerging enormous window, in order to get an even better view of what was being so dramatically unveiled before his very eyes.

'Is that—?' he started to ask.

'Earth?' finished the Chief Inspector.

'That's the one,' replied Capstan.

'It most certainly is!' and the Chief Inspector stood up to join him. As they both stared out at it, he said 'Believe it or not, we're currently travelling at over 6,800 miles an hour, and are being kept in geostationary orbit over the UKA at a distance of only about two hundred and fifty miles, which puts us in the perfect position to keep an eye on the place.'

'The UKA?' asked Capstan.

'That's right, the UKA. Don't you recognise it?'

'Don't you mean the UK?' he asked, clearly confused.

'Ah, sorry. My fault. I completely forgot. Understandably you're a little behind the times. America took over the world some time ago, so what was called the United Kingdom back then has since become the United Kingdom of America.'

'America took over the world?' repeated Capstan, with total and complete incredulity.

'Back in 2341.'

'My God! I must admit that I always thought it would be China who'd take over the world,' said Capstan, still gazing out. 'Them or the North Koreans.'

'It was before my time,' said the Chief Inspector, 'but it was when our great leader, President Müller, won the US election that he took overall control of Earth, and for the better, I may add.'

'President Müller?' asked Capstan, staring at the man beside him. 'You mean President Dick Müller? That fat orange guy with the dodgy wig? The one who won the American Presidency back in my time?'

'Oh no, no, no. He's long gone. I'm talking about what must be his great grandson, Dick Müller IV.'

As Capstan's brain did the maths on that one, he eventually asked, 'But, even so, how could his great grandson be President of America in the year 2459?'

'Er, because he won the election,' answered the Chief Inspector, wondering if this Capstan chap did have his full complement of marbles after all.

'But that would make him over three-hundred years old, wouldn't it?'

'I've no idea how old he is,' replied the Chief Inspector. 'He must be getting on, I suppose, but I suspect that life expectancy has risen a fair bit since your time. It's certainly fairly normal for people to live that long these days, assuming he is three hundred years old, that is.'

'B-but—three hundred years old?'

'Yes, well, I'd say that that's about average.'

'About average!?!' exclaimed Capstan. 'But—how?'

'Oh it's all fairly straight forward. When one of your body parts wears out, you just upgrade it for a new one. Your leg is a good example of that.'

'Oh,' said Capstan. 'So the Earth must have become even more over-populated than it was when I was there?'

'Perhaps.'

'And it's since become a dystopian concrete jungle in which the inhabitants spend their days fighting over the last scraps of food?'

'Not at all!' exclaimed the Chief Inspector, clearly horrified by the idea. 'There's always been more than enough to go around, probably even in your day. It's just that back then I suspect it was never managed effectively. Probably a question of too many cooks.'

'Too many cooks?' asked Capstan, wondering if Bake Off had become so popular that the entire population of Earth now spent their days making cakes.

'Yes, you know. Too many leaders trying to run too many countries, and always at the expense of everyone else. Fortunately, President Müller changed all that.'

'By taking over the world?'

'That's right. Once he'd done that, it became a much more organised sort of planet to live on.'

'I see,' said Capstan, gazing back down at Earth. 'It's funny, but I'd always thought that someone taking over the world would've been a bad thing.'

'Really?' asked the Chief Inspector. 'How strange! I can't imagine why.'

'So, how did he do it?' asked Capstan, out of curiosity.

'How did he do what?'

'Take over the world?'

'Oh, that! Well, again it was before my time, but the history books say that one day all the various countries' leaders sat around a giant table in the shape of a tortoise shell and decided to put him in charge.'

'Really?' Capstan had heard a number of truly hard to believe things since waking up, but that one really took the biscuit.

Sensing his doubt, the Chief Inspector said, 'I suspect they were getting rather desperate. It was around the time of the Great Depletion.'

'The Great Depletion?' repeated Capstan.

'When the oil ran out,' clarified the Chief Inspector.

'Oh, I see. Well, I suppose that does make more sense.'

'And once they'd all agreed that he should take over the world, he simply divided it up into regions, giving each one its own responsibility. Here, let me show you,' and he pulled out what looked like an iPhone, very similar to the one the doctor had had, and after a few swipes he held it out, and a perfect hologram of Earth appeared above it, as if by magic.

'Here's the United States of America,' he started, pointing at the North American continent. 'They're responsible for Design and Creativity. Up here is the United Canada of America, that's where all the scientists live.' Moving the globe around with his finger, he continued, 'Over here is the United Europe of America. They do all the management and legal stuff. Here's the United Asian Continent of America. They deal with manufacture. Down here is the United African Continent of America, who look after the world's solar energy supply. Over here is the United Australasian Continent of America, responsible for food and drink, and all the way down here, right at the bottom is the United Antarctic Continent of America, who supply the planet's wind energy. Apparently it blows a gale down there, although I've never been.'

'And what about us?' asked Capstan, who couldn't help but be impressed at how well everything had been organised.

'Ah yes, the United Kingdom of America. Well, we have probably the most important job of all; that of dairy production.'

'Dairy production?' repeated Capstan, as he seemed to have found himself doing rather a lot recently.

'Yes, you know: the production of milk, primarily, although we also make yoghurt, butter and cheese.'

'And that's important, is it?'

'Sorry, of course. I keep forgetting that you've missed the last four hundred and fifty years. Since we began trading with other planets, the demand for milk has increased exponentially, as has its value; and it's become the universe's most in-demand resource. And as we're the only planet in the universe known to be able to produce the stuff, apart from Titan of course, the United Kingdom of America has the largest Gross Domestic Product of any of the other states.'

'Titan?' asked Capstan.

'Yes, Titan, but their milk doesn't have nearly the high ratio of cream that ours does, and you certainly can't make cheese and yoghurt out if it.'

By now, Capstan was experiencing serious information overload. Not only had he just learnt that America had taken over the world, and that they'd done a remarkably good job of it, but also that milk had become a scarce natural resource which was in heavy demand by intelligent alien life throughout the universe that up until then he didn't even know existed. It was all just too much for his brain to handle, and he certainly wasn't being given enough time to process it all. So he just started to stare at the Chief Inspector, with a completely blank look about him.

Sensing that he may have relayed too much information too quickly, for the human brain at least, the Chief Inspector put his iPhone thing away and said, 'Anyway, that's not what I wanted to talk to you about.'

'It wasn't?' asked Capstan.

'Not really. I actually invited you here because I have a proposition for you.'

'For me?' asked Capstan again.

'Yes, for you,' and he placed a reassuring hand on his guest's shoulder to lead him back towards his desk. 'I've been looking through your files. It's impressive stuff! That OBE thing, and not one but two Queen's Police Medals for Gallantry and Distinguished Service. Quite remarkable!'

Capstan found himself walking just a little bit taller.

'So, anyway, now that you're here, and that we're unfortunately unable to send you back, I was wondering if you'd like to pick up where you left off?'

'Sorry, but how do you mean?'

'By getting back to work, as a detective inspector for the UKA's Space Police.'

'Oh, um…' replied Capstan, who hadn't had a chance to think about what he was going to do for a job yet. But now that it looked like he was going to have to live in the 25th Century on a permanent basis, it was probably something he should begin to consider.

Stepping back behind his desk, the Chief Inspector added, 'I've been able to dig up your old employment contract. It doesn't seem to have ever been terminated, so you're actually still a detective inspector, and that means it would be a remarkably straight forward process to get you back to work. You wouldn't even have to sign anything!'

'Well, I don't know,' said Capstan, unsure if he really wanted to spend the remainder of his days being a policeman, again, especially if his life expectancy in the 25th Century had more than tripled, meaning that he could end up being stuck doing the same job for the next three hundred years.

'We'd give you a pay rise, obviously,' added the Chief Inspector, 'and you could even work alongside Lieutenant Bushdew, just like the old days!'

The Chief Inspector presumably thought that offering Dewbush as his lieutenant would be an incentive, which he probably wouldn't have done had he known about the working relationship Capstan had had with the man's great-great-great-great-grandfather, who'd been permanently at least one sandwich short of a picnic, but most of the time more like two.

'Well, I, er…'

'Great! That's settled then. You can pick up your badge from the duty sergeant, along with your touch-tech and a gun.'

'A gun!' exclaimed Capstan. As a former British policeman he'd never even touched a gun before.

'And here's your first case,' he continued. 'I'll send it to Bushdew for now,' and he swiped the top of the desk again, but outwards this time, and in the direction of Dewbush. At the same time, Dewbush's watch pinged and he pulled out what looked very much like an iPhone from his inside suit jacket pocket to give the new case file a quick courtesy glance.

'A missing cow case?' Dewbush asked, moments later, seemingly quite surprised. 'Are you sure, sir?'

'Yes, I know it's a bit of a step up for you, Bushdew, but with Detective Inspector Capstan here to help lead the way, I've no doubt you'll be able to handle it.'

With that, the Chief Inspector touched his seemingly invisible desk and called out, 'Susan, could you show Detective Inspector Capstan and Lieutenant Bushdew out for me, please?'

'Right away, Chief Inspector.'

'Well, good luck, gentlemen,' said the Chief Inspector as he looked from Capstan to Dewbush, 'and I look forward to hearing how you get on with that missing cow case. But if you could have it solved by the end of the day, that would be appreciated.'

CHAPTER SEVEN

'ALL RIGHT, Bushdew, how's it going, mate?'
'Hello, Murbles. Very well, thank you,' said
Dewbush, as he and Capstan arrived at the Duty
Sergeant's desk, an object that was about chest high,
had smooth polished white sides, and which to
Capstan's relief he could actually see.

'Who's this then?' asked the man Dewbush called
Murbles, and who Capstan assumed was the Duty
Sergeant.

'This is Detective Inspector Capstan,' said
Dewbush, adding, 'He's from the 21st Century!'

Now that Dewbush had found himself assigned to
work under this highly-decorated man from Earth's
distant past, he'd become quite excited by the idea.

'The 21st Century, eh?' said Murbles, as he looked
Capstan up and down. 'I hear that Earth was a right
dump back then.'

Capstan, meanwhile, had found himself taking an
immediate dislike to this ill-spoken, short, largely
unattractive man who was wearing a normal white
office shirt with a black tie which had been left
undone. Like the other men he'd met so far Murbles
had beige-coloured skin and mousey-brown hair, but
unlike everyone else he clearly hadn't shaved for a few

53

days, and he didn't look like he'd bothered even to brush his hair. And Capstan's instinctive feelings against this unkempt man weren't helped by the fact that he'd just insulted his former home, or at least the bygone era of when he used to live on it.

'It wasn't *that* bad,' replied Capstan although, compared to how the Chief Inspector had described Earth to him in its present form, it probably had been.

'He's been re-commissioned to work for us,' said Dewbush, 'so Chapwick told me to bring him down here to pick up a badge, along with his touch-tech, and a gun.'

The Duty Sergeant looked back at Capstan. 'I suppose I'd better take a photo of you then, hadn't I?' he said, and reached under the desk to retrieve yet another iPhone-looking thing which he held up to take Capstan's picture.

Having done so, he stared at the screen. 'That will do,' he said. 'And how do you spell Catspam?'

'Oh, it's actually Cap*stan*,' said Capstan. 'C-A-P-S-T-A-N.'

'And you're a Detective Inspector?' asked the Duty Sergeant, as he began tapping at the smartphone's surface with his thumbs.

'That's correct, yes.'

After a few moments, a beeping noise came from behind the desk somewhere, and reaching down, Murbles pulled up a fully laminated UKA Space Police

ID, along with a black leather wallet.

Slotting one inside the other, he turned it over to show where a highly polished, chrome-plated badge stood out on the other side, with the words SPACE POLICE over the top of an embossed five-pointed star, and UKA in smaller letters underneath.

'Here you go,' said Murbles, handing it to Capstan.

Taking it, Capstan was almost looking forward to becoming an actual, real-life space policeman, and after he'd turned it over a few times he opened it up to look at the ID inside.

'Excuse me,' he said, 'but this says Detective Inspector Catspam?'

'That's what you said, wasn't it?'

'Er, no, I said Cap*stan!*'

'Close enough.'

'Sorry, but what do you mean, "close enough"?'

'Look, honestly mate, nobody's going to look at it.'

'That's hardly the point though, is it? You've clearly spelt my name wrong!'

Murbles looked at the ID again. 'It's only a bit wrong.'

'Well, can you change it, please? I can't go around being called Catspam all the time.'

'Too late, mate. I've laminated it now,' and as if to change the subject, he pushed on, 'Anyway, here's your gun,' and he reached underneath the desk again to heave out what looked like a Nerf gun in every way, shape and form, except for the fact that it was a metallic black colour, instead of blue and orange, and looked as if it weighed a fair bit more as well.

Having placed that down, he reached back under the desk. 'And here are fifty rounds of 12mm armour piercing, self-guiding cartridges with impact-exploding tips.' He slammed a box down on the desk, although with a little too much force for Capstan's liking. 'And here's your police frequency touch-tech,' which seemed to consist of a watch like Dewbush's along with the same iPhone device that everyone seemed to have, and a pair of sunglasses.

Capstan wasn't looking at the watch, or the iPhone. He'd even forgotten about his miss-spelt Space Police ID. All he could do was stare at the gun.

'What am I going to do with *that?*' he asked, pointing at it.

'I think the idea is that you shoot people with it, normally when they're running away,' said Murbles.

'But…where am I going to put it?' asked Capstan, desperate to think of an excuse not to take it. 'It's hardly going to fit down my trousers.'

'Oh, sorry. I forgot.' Reaching under the desk again, Murbles said, 'Here's your holster,' and he placed a black leather shoulder-holster alongside everything else.

'The gun is the MDK 12mm Decapitator,' said Dewbush, picking it up for Capstan to have a closer look. He passed it to him, saying, 'I've got the same model,' and opened up his shiny suit jacket to reveal an identical one nestled under his left arm.

'But—I've never had a gun before,' said Capstan, feeling its weight in his hand.

'Don't worry,' said Dewbush, 'I'll show you how to use it at some point. Anyway, we'd better be off,' and with that he gathered up all the other items from off the desk on Capstan's behalf, saying to Murbles, 'We've been given a case of a missing cow!' as he did so.

'A missing cow, eh!' exclaimed the Duty Sergeant.

'And Chapwick wants it solved by the end of the day.'

'Really? Well, good luck with *that!*'

With a concerned look, Dewbush said, 'Thanks, Murbles. See you later.'

'Have a good one, Bushdew.'

'If you could follow me, Detective Inspector, sir,' said Dewbush, with a level of respect Capstan was more used to, 'I'll take you down to the docking bay where our car is parked.'

CHAPTER EIGHT

THE DOCKING BAY was located in the depths of UKA's Police Station 999, one floor up from the deep space storage level where Capstan had been kept in a state of suspended animation for more years than he could remember, literally, and which was where they kept everything they didn't really need but thought they'd better keep hold of, like traffic cones, and prisoners. Although very useful on Earth, traffic cones had proved to be worse than useless in space. They simply didn't stay where they were left. The UKA's Space Police had a similar problem with their prisoners, but that wasn't unique to them. Throughout time, prisoners rarely stayed where they were told to, especially human ones, which was why any they had knocking about the place were kept locked up in storage.

To reach the docking bay, Dewbush ushered Capstan into the same lift they'd used to see the Chief Inspector, but headed down instead of up.

Despite it being a journey of some twenty six floors, it took less than ten seconds for them to get there, yet Capstan hadn't even felt as if he'd gone anywhere at all. In fact, the only way he knew he was going down was because of an orange illuminated panel, whose light descended alongside a column of thirty numbers which Capstan assumed marked how many levels there were in total.

Stepping out of the lift, Capstan walked straight out into an immense open plan area that seemed to be some kind of giant-sized aircraft hangar, crammed full with dozens upon dozens of police vans, similar in shape and size to the ones back in his day, the only discernible difference being that they didn't seem to have any wheels. The place was an absolute hive of activity, which was quite a shock for him. Up until then, everywhere Capstan had been taken to had been quiet and relatively devoid of people, but here there were hundreds of space police personnel, some in uniform, and others in grease-splattered overalls who Capstan assumed to be the mechanics. There was one thing about them that was the same; they all had beige skin with sandy coloured hair, just like Dewbush's, the Commissioner's, and the Duty Sergeant's.

'Doesn't the Space Police employ ethnic minorities?' asked Capstan, watching in awe as a police van over to his left rose up about a metre from the ground where it hovered, momentarily, before slowly turning a full 180 degrees and drifting off towards what Capstan had at first thought was just a vast black wall. But when the police van didn't stop at the wall, and instead drove straight into it, he realised that it wasn't a wall at all, but was in fact space.

'Sorry, sir,' said Dewbush, 'I can't say that I've heard of anyone called Ethnic Minority before. Was he a friend of yours?'

Capstan turned and narrowed his eyes at him, but it really didn't look as if Dewbush was being sarcastic. He simply didn't seem to have ever heard of the phrase "ethnic minority" before.

'Shall I look him up for you, sir?' offered Dewbush, reaching inside his jacket, presumably for his iPhone touch-tech thing.

'No, it's OK.'

'I don't mind, sir.'

'Really, it's fine, Dewbush. He's probably dead by now anyway.'

'You're probably right, sir. I doubt if there's anyone who was born in the 21st Century who's still alive, apart from you, of course, sir,' and Dewbush gave Capstan a brief sympathetic look, before turning away.

'Our car is just over here, sir,' and he led Capstan to the far right side of the hanger, past more white vans, where there were indeed a number of sleek-looking vehicles that were all the same gun metal grey colour, not the rather more obvious white with chequered blue and yellow squares of the space police vans. Through Capstan's eyes, the dark grey cars looked like all-terrain versions of an Audi TT which had been left parked outside a London housing estate overnight, as none of them had any wheels.

'Shall we head off, sir?' asked Dewbush, as he opened the right hand side door.

'Er, I don't suppose I could ask where we're going, before we go?' asked Capstan, as he glanced down into the car and then out, over towards the black wall where the endless nothingness of the universe seemed to begin.

'Earth, sir.'

'Oh. I see,' said Capstan. 'Any particular part?' he asked.

To be honest, now that he was standing beside an actual Space Police car, being invited to climb inside for a trip out into actual space, he was having second thoughts about the whole thing, and was wondering if there were any jobs available in admin.

'It's a dairy farm on the south coast of the UKA, sir, but don't worry. I have the address and postcode.'

'I see,' said Capstan. 'I don't suppose I could go to the loo first?'

'We can stop off at Orion's Seatbelt service station on the way, sir.'

'How about something to eat? I still haven't had any lunch.'

'We'll be able to pick up some sandwiches there as well, sir.'

'Maybe I should have a go with that gun?' asked Capstan, glancing down at the weapon that was still in his hand. 'Just in case I need to use it.'

'It's unlikely that you will, sir. Not today, at least.'

'How about a coffee then?'

'Again, we can get one from the service station, sir,' and with that, Dewbush stood to one side and invited Capstan in to what he hoped was the passenger seat.

CHAPTER NINE

O NCE INSIDE THE unmarked Space Police car, after Capstan and Dewbush had both closed their air-tight doors and had put their seat belts on, Dewbush pressed a red button on the dashboard beside a very normal-looking steering wheel, and the car's GPS asked them for their destination.

'Port's Mouth, please,' replied Dewbush.

Capstan turned to stare at his brand new subordinate as the car sought clarification by asking, '*Did you mean Port's Mouth, the United States of America, or Port's Mouth, the United Kingdom of America?*'

'Port's Mouth, the United Kingdom of America, please?'

'*OK, your destination is Port's Mouth in the United Kingdom of America. Please state the postcode for Port's Mouth, the United Kingdom of America.*'

Dewbush pulled out his touch-tech, swiped at the screen a few times to find the missing cow report that Chief Inspector Chapwick had sent him, before reading out just as clearly as he possibly could, 'PO1 4EX 7EY.'

'*Thank you! You said, 'PO1 4BX 7BY. Please say "yes" to confirm your destination's postcode, or "no" to say that that is not the correct destination postcode.*'

'No,' said Dewbush, as the GPS had mistaken the E's for B's, as it did have a tendency to do.

'OK, please repeat the postcode for Port's Mouth in the United Kingdom of America.'

'PO1 4*EX* 7*EY*,' repeated Dewbush, placing a firm emphasis on the letters "E".

'Thank you!' said the car's GPS. *'You said, PO1 4BX 7BY. Please say "yes" to confirm your destination's postcode, or "no" to say that that is not the correct destination postcode.'*

With an apologetic tone, Dewbush turned to Capstan and said, 'Sorry about this, sir. I won't be a moment,' before he continued trying to relate the correct postcode by looking at the dashboard and repeating, 'PO1 4*EX* 7*EY*.'

'Thank you!' said the car's GPS system once again. 'You said, 'PO1 4BX 7BY. Please say "yes" to confirm your destination's postcode, or "no" to say that that is not the correct destination postcode.'

'NO!' said Dewbush, with a raised voice. He was clearly becoming a little irritated.

'OK, please repeat the postcode for Port's Mouth in the United Kingdom of America.'

'Do you often have this problem?' asked Capstan, who'd been waiting patiently for the opportunity to ask Dewbush to clarify that they were indeed going to Portsmouth, the place he'd known well, as that was where he'd spent so many years working as a detective inspector and which, over the four centuries he'd been in a state of suspended animation, must have reverted back to the name given to it by the Saxons.

'Unfortunately I do, sir. We're still awaiting our GPS voice activation systems to be upgraded, but with the latest round of public sector cutbacks, it may be a while until we get it. I'll give it one more go, sir, if you could just bear with me,' and with that he turned back to the dashboard, and said, 'PO1 4EX 7EY, the "E's" are as in elephant, not "B's" as in Bertie.'

There was a momentary pause before the GPS system came back with, '*I'm sorry, I did not recognise the postcode PO1 4BX 7BY the B's are as in elephant not B as in Bertie. Is it in Port's Mouth, the United States of America, or Port's Mouth, the United Kingdom of America?*'

'I'm going to have to enter it manually,' said Dewbush, and leaned forward to use the touch-tech display mounted on the dashboard, just above what looked like a CD player.

Moments later the GPS said, '*Thank you!*' and with reassuring confidence, added, '*Your route is being calculated!*'

As he waited for it to do that, Dewbush adjusted his rear view mirror before turning to Capstan and asking, 'Are you ready, sir?'

'Not really,' replied Capstan, as he checked that his seatbelt's buckle was secure, that his door was firmly closed and that there wasn't a gap around the top of the window.

As Capstan felt the car lift up in the most disconcerting way, the GPS piped up with, '*After three hundred yards, turn left!*' and the car began to gently float its way forward, heading slowly towards the hangar's edge and the dense, all-consuming blackness of space beyond.

'I assume this is safe, and everything?' asked Capstan, as he held on to the edge of his seat, as if beginning the ascent of some dodgy rollercoaster ride which was missing the bar that was supposed to stop him from being hurled out when rounding a corner.

'How do you mean, sir?'

'You know. Policemen travelling around in space and everything. It's been done before, I take it?' asked Capstan, staring straight ahead.

'Er, of course, sir. Many times.'

Interrupting their conversation, the GPS said, '*After 200 yards, turn left!*'

'How many times, exactly?' continued Capstan.

'I'm not sure, sir, but certainly quite a few.'

'And nobody gets killed doing it?' asked Capstan.

'Gets killed, sir?'

'You know, like when something goes wrong, and they end up dead?'

'Um,' said Dewbush. 'I don't think so, sir. At least, not very often.'

As the car continued to float ever nearer the blackness beyond, the GPS said, '*After 100 yards, turn left!*

'Sorry, but did you say, "not very often"?' asked Capstan.

'That's right, sir.'

'Do you know how often?'

'You mean exactly, sir?'

'Well no, but a rough estimate?'

'I'm not sure, sir. Every now and again, I suppose.'

'I see,' said Capstan, who couldn't help but notice that they were about to leave the relative safety of the police space station for what Capstan had always been told was an extremely hazardous place for humans, being that space didn't have an atmosphere, which apparently made breathing in and out rather difficult.

'I don't suppose there's any chance you could let me out, is there?'

Dewbush glanced over at Capstan with a confused look, before saying, 'Ah, I get it now, sir. You're "joking"!'

'Honestly, Dewbush, I'm not. Please let me out!' begged Capstan, just as the GPS said, *Turn left!*

'We did the 21st Century at school, sir,' began Dewbush in a conversational tone, as he did what the GPS had told him to do and turned left. 'Our history teacher said that you used to spend a lot of time taking part in "joking" and "larking around".'

'And you're telling me that you don't?' asked Capstan, finding himself momentarily distracted from the prospect of entering space for the very first time.

'Of course not, sir.'

'And why's that? I suppose the human species has evolved beyond the need to have a sense of humour?'

'Nothing like that, sir. I think it was just considered to be too dangerous, sir.'

'Too dangerous?'

'That's right, sir. My teacher said that it became increasingly difficult to know if someone was joking or if they were being serious, and the situation rapidly declined when the world's politicians began saying things they didn't actually mean.'

'I thought that's what all politicians did,' said Capstan. 'Back in my day I seem to remember it was called lying.'

'Lying, sir?'

'Yes, you know. When someone says something that isn't true.'

'I see, sir. But I thought that was called joking, sir?'

'No, Dewbush. You're thinking of sarcasm. Joking is when you say something that's funny. Whether it's true or not is largely irrelevant.'

'I see, sir. So, what's sarcasm then?'

'Sarcasm is when you say something you don't mean, but you say it in such a way that it's obvious you didn't mean it.'

'But…' began Dewbush, 'how does that differ from lying, sir?'

'Lying, Dewbush, is when you say something that isn't true, whereas sarcasm is, well... I suppose sarcasm is also saying something that isn't true, but the difference is that when you're being sarcastic, you're saying it in such a way that the person you're saying it to is supposed to realise that you're not being serious.'

Dewbush shook his head with confusion. He'd been unable to understand the difference between lying, joking and sarcasm when he'd been taught about them at school, and this conversation with a man who'd actually come from the era when society had used all three with apparent gay abandon hadn't helped. In fact, he was probably now even more confused. So, to hopefully end the subject, he said, 'Anyway, sir, it's illegal now, so it probably doesn't matter.'

'Sorry, what's illegal?'

'Joking, sir.'

Dewbush turned to stare at Dewbush. 'You're telling me that telling a joke is now illegal?' he asked, struggling to believe what he'd just been told.

'Yes, sir, although only in public places. I think you're still allowed to joke in your own home, sir.'

'What about sarcasm?' asked Capstan.

'Oh, that's illegal as well, sir.'

'That's a shame.'

'Why's that, sir? Did you used to be sarcasmastic?'

'It was called being sarcastic, Dewbush, but no. I

only used it in extreme circumstances, normally when having to make conversation with your great-great-great-great-grandfather.'

There was a lull in the conversation before Dewbush asked, 'What was he like, sir?'

'Who, your great-great-great-great-grandfather?'

'Yes, him, sir.'

'He was a complete—'

Capstan was about to say that he was a complete twat, but before he said it he decided that it would probably be disrespectful to the memory of his former sergeant, and could also upset his great-great-great-great-grandson, the young man sitting next to him. So, instead he said, 'He was a completely brilliant policeman, and one who will be sorely missed.'

'Was he, sir?'

'Not really,' and keen to change the subject himself, said, 'So, we're in space now, are we?'

CHAPTER TEN

A S CAPSTAN AND DEWBUSH began their descent towards the United Kingdom of America, and a city called Port's Mouth situated on its south coast, the President of Earth, Dick Müller IV, currently aged two hundred and ninety three, was having breakfast on the Truman Balcony of the White House. This was his favourite place to have breakfast as it was situated on the second floor, giving him a clear unobstructed view of the south lawn, or what he called his backyard. There he could spend a few minutes each day in quiet, peaceful meditation as he ploughed his way through an All American Breakfast, normally served with extra pancakes soaked in maple syrup, and all washed down with a well-big Americano coffee.

Standing just to the side of him and wearing a transparent nightie was his wife. Well, effectively she was, but he wasn't married to her. She wasn't even human. She was a Wife-bot Series 4000, the very latest in advanced humanoid robotics who he called Susan, or Darling, or Love Puppet, or Bad Bedroom Bonk Bunny depending on the circumstances, or the position he'd managed to get her into at the time. And although it had recently become legal for humans to marry humanoids, he hadn't done. He wasn't prepared to make that sort of commitment to her, and besides, he'd been married thirty-two times before, and divorced thirty-two times shortly afterwards, and the novelty factor had worn off several decades earlier.

'Is your breakfast nice, Darling?' asked Susan, in a soothing rhythmic tone.

'Very nice, thank you,' he answered, between mouthfuls.

'Can I get you anything else, Darling?' she asked, as she stood there, watching him eat.

'No, thank you. This is just great!'

'More coffee, perhaps, Darling?'

'I've still not finished this one, but thanks for asking.'

He didn't need to be quite so polite to her all the time; after all, she was only a robot, but there was something about her that he couldn't quite put his finger on, and wasn't too keen to find out what would happen if he managed to upset her.

'How about an extra sausage, Darling?'

'Again, no. I've got four already, and you've cooked them to perfection!'

'There's more toast, if you'd like, Darling.'

'Really, I'm fine, thank you.'

'How about a hand-job when you've finished, Darling?'

At that precise moment, the President's Chief of

Staff, Gavin Sherburt, poked his head around the balcony's French doors, cleared his throat rather obviously, and asked, 'Are you ready for our meeting, Mr President?'

'I'm still eating breakfast, Gavin.'

'I can come back later if you like, Mr President.'

'Yes, please,' said President Müller, who'd just started looking forward to getting a hand-job from his sexy new Wife-bot, who'd come with a vibrating right hand that had no less than five speed settings, making it perfect for carnal stress relief in the bedroom, and which she probably found quite useful in the kitchen, when making a cake, for example.

'Righty-ho!' said Gavin, still hovering besides the French doors. 'So, when do you think I should come back, Mr President? It's just that you're supposed to be spending the day with Lord Von Splotitty, and we still need to agree on the agenda.'

Swallowing a fried egg, President Müller asked, 'Who the hell is Lord Von Splotitty?'

Actually he knew exactly who Lord Von Splotitty was, but never liked to admit it, not even to his Chief of Staff, despite the fact that he'd been the subject of countless highly-classified discussions.

'Er, he's the Supreme High Councillor of Titan, Mr President. The Commander-in-Chief of the Mammary Clans. He's here for the Intergalactic Dairy Produce Trade Talks.'

'Oh, you mean Tim McTitty Head.'

'I thought we agreed, Mr President, that we weren't going to call him that.'

'I'm fairly sure, Gavin, we agreed that we *were* going to call him that, and for the obvious reason that he looks exactly like a big giant tit. In fact, now that I think about it, they all do, don't you think?'

'If you say so, Mr President.'

'And it is today that he's coming, is it?'

Again, he knew that he was due to arrive that morning.

'He is, Mr President.'

'And you want to go over the agenda?'

'I would like to, yes, Mr President.'

'Tell you what, Gavin. Just bring Mr McTitty Head up to the Oval Office, I'll meet him, say hello, and you can take it from there. OK?'

'No problem at all, Mr President, but at what time?'

'What time would you suggest?'

'Could we say… nine-forty, Mr President?'

'Tell you what, let's say ten, shall we?'

'Absolutely, Mr President. And you're happy for the press to be in attendance?'

'I suppose.'

'And what about afterwards, Mr President?'

'What about afterwards?'

'What should I do with him after you've met him and shaken his tentacle-hand thing in front of the press, Mr President?'

'I really don't care, Gavin, but make sure that by the end of the day he's completely drunk. And once he is, just shove him into the Lincoln Bedroom suite with a few prostitutes, as we've discussed, and film him in action. I'll then be able to tell him first thing tomorrow morning that if he doesn't hand over Titan to us, we'll be showing the video to his wife and children, and anyone else who's interested, like the rest of the Galaxy, for example.'

'And you really think that will work, do you, Mr President?'

'Of course it will work, Gavin!'

'But how can you be so sure, Mr President?'

'Listen, Gavin, I'll let you into a little secret. I know it was a bit before your time, but that's basically how I took over the World. So yes, I'm one hundred percent confident that it will work.'

'I see, Mr President,' said Gavin, who just stood there digesting that hitherto unknown piece of information whilst his boss, the President of Earth and Commander-in-Chief of all of its military forces, ingested a sausage.

'But I thought,' continued Gavin, 'you took over the World because all the great leaders sat around a table that was in the shape of a giant tortoise shell, where they came to the decision that you were the best man for the job of becoming their leader?'

'Yes, that's right, they did,' replied President Müller, as he loaded up a fork with an entire pancake. 'But the night before, I got them all drunk, shoved them into a room full of prostitutes, had them all filmed, and then threatened to show the various videos to their families unless they did.'

'Oh, I see, Mr President. Sorry, I didn't know that.'

'I'm pleased to hear it! It's highly classified. If you had known, I'd have had you killed a very long time ago.'

Gavin gulped. He didn't doubt that for a second. President Müller had a reputation for having people killed, and for a lot less than knowing something they shouldn't. But that did place him in rather an awkward position, and choosing his words very carefully, he asked, 'But you've, er, told me now, Mr President, so I, er, hope you're not going to, er…?'

'Have you killed?'

'Well, er, yes, Mr President.'

'Don't be stupid. You're my Chief of Staff now, and I certainly can't be bothered to find another one.'

'Yes, of course, Mr President. Thank you, Mr President.'

'Don't mention it. Now, run along, and if you bring Lord Von McTitty Head, or whatever his name is, to the Oval Office for ten, I'll do my best to give his tentacle thing a shake in front of the press for you.'

'That's very kind of you, Mr President, and thank

you again.'

CHAPTER ELEVEN

AFTER CAPSTAN AND DEWBUSH had stopped off at the nearby Orion's Belt service station, filled the car up with hydrogen and bought some sandwiches along with two well-big Americano Coffees, they'd had to spend over an hour drifting down through Earth's atmosphere, which at least had given them time to eat what had turned out to be a very late lunch.

It had also given Dewbush the chance to give Capstan his touch-tech equipment, as well as his gun's shoulder holster, and explain to him why they had to re-enter the Earth's atmosphere so slowly, which was apparently to prevent isentropic heating of the air molecules as they did, something that was vitally important as the car only had a cheap moulded plastic bumper which would have melted otherwise.

So it wasn't until a little after four o'clock that they reached what used to be known as Portsmouth, but to Capstan's eyes now bore a closer resemblance to a futuristic version of Tokyo, so much so that he nearly asked if the GPS had taken them to the wrong side of the planet. But then he spotted the Spinnaker Tower, Portsmouth's famous landmark observation point that had little practical use in the 21st Century, but now looked as if it was being used as a multi-storey car park by some of the many hundreds upon hundreds of flying cars, buses and trucks that seemed to be endlessly circling the city like a kettle of hungry vultures, waiting for something on the ground to keel over and die.

Ten minutes later the GPS piped up with, '*You have reached your destination!*' and Dewbush landed the car in the relatively small customer car park of somewhere called Butterbum Farm, although it didn't look much like a farm in that it wasn't surrounded by rolling hills of lush green grass grazed by herds of wandering farm-type animals. Instead there was just a large shed with a corrugated iron roof and a small building next to that, above which was a sign that said Butterbum Farm Shop.

Relieved to have landed safely, and after Dewbush had shown him how to open his door, Capstan stepped out only to be hit by a wall of heat, which was so intense that it felt as if it was burning the insides of his nostrils whenever he breathed in.

'My god, Dewbush! Are you sure this is England?' he asked.

'Er, no, sir,' said Dewbush, as he closed the driver's side door. 'This is Port's Mouth. Did you want to go to a place called England?'

Ignoring the question, Capstan said, 'When the hell did it get so damned hot?'

'Er…' answered Dewbush.

Resisting the urge to undo his collar, Capstan said, 'I suppose this is the result of four hundred and fifty years of Global Warming?'

'I don't think so, sir. It's always been like this, in the summer at least.'

'Not when I lived here it wasn't!'

'Really, sir?'

'Yes, really, Dewbush. This feels more like the Gobi Desert!'

'Was that a restaurant, sir?'

'No, of course it wasn't a restaurant!'

Deciding that it kind of sounded like his new boss was keen to know the weather forecast, Dewbush pulled out his touch-tech PalmPad from out of his inside suit jacket pocket.

'It's currently thirty-six degrees Celsius, sir, which apparently is well below average for the time of year.'

'And what's average, dare I ask?'

'Forty-one, sir.'

'You're joking!'

'Of course not, sir. As a lieutenant within the UKA Space Police, I'm duty bound never to joke, sir.'

'It was just a figure of speech, Dewbush. I didn't mean that you were actually telling a joke.'

'I see, sir,' said Dewbush, but without looking as if he did. 'Anyway, sir,' he continued, keen to move the subject away from the telling of jokes, something that could easily cost him his job if he was caught doing it, not to mention getting him five years in prison, 'we're supposed to be meeting the Farm Manager.'

'Does he have a name?' asked Capstan, closing the passenger door.

'He's actually a she, sir,' said Dewbush. 'Miss Butterbum. Lucy Butterbum, to be precise.'

'How unfortunate for her,' said Capstan, as he wondered how he was going to cope with having to work in such extreme heat.

'How do you mean, sir?'

'Never mind,' replied Capstan. So far, Dewbush's apparent inability to understand the concept of humour in any of its many guises only served to remind him of his great-great-great-great-grandfather, who'd had a similar problem.

'She's probably the daughter of the farm's owner,' continued Capstan.

'What makes you say that, sir?'

'Er…because of the surname, Dewbush.'

'The surname, sir?'

Capstan stared over at his young subordinate. Not only did he share his former sergeant's facial features, and a total and complete inability to understand satire, it was becoming increasingly obvious that he also shared his extraordinary lack of ability for deductive reasoning.

'Her surname, Dewbush. Butterbum. It's the same

81

name as the farm.'

'Oh, I see what you mean, sir.'

Shaking his head, Capstan thought he better start taking the lead in this investigation, else it was probably unlikely they'd make it beyond the farm's carpark. 'Shall we take a look around?' he suggested.

'Good idea, sir. Miss Butterbum must be here somewhere!'

It was odd, but despite finding himself in Earth's far distant future, in a virtually unrecognisable city that was insanely hot and within which everyone he'd ever known was—to the best of his knowledge at least— dead, he was beginning to feel right at home.

Without further ado, Capstan headed straight over to the shop, where he thought it most likely to find someone who might know the whereabouts of the Farm Manager.

Pushing open the door, Capstan found the shop itself to have an almost rustic feel to it, a bit like the charity shops he'd known from his former life, the most obvious difference being that instead of selling a lot of unwanted junk and dead people's clothes, it only appeared to sell milk. And there wasn't an old lady sitting behind the counter, staring at a calculator, hoping to God that nobody would ask her an overly complex question like, 'How much is this?' Instead, there was a beautiful and incredibly lifelike female humanoid robot which had sparkling blue eyes and long blonde hair that hung in plaits on either side of her head. She was dressed in a very sexy 19th Century Milk Maid costume, which had a distinctly low-cut frilly white blouse with a black Basque on top that supported a quite remarkable pair of generously proportioned breasts. But despite the realistic nature of the robot, it appeared to be off-line, as it stared out at nothing, without either moving or blinking, very much like a teenager would have done who'd been forced to work in a similar job.

When Dewbush came into the shop behind him, Capstan said, 'I think this one's batteries have run out.'

Looking at the robot in question, Dewbush said, 'It's a Retail-Bot, sir. They go offline if they're not busy. If you say, "Excuse me", quite loudly, sir, it should come back online.'

'Oh, I see,' said Capstan. 'Thank you, lieutenant,' and he leaned in towards the sexy robot's head and shouted, 'EXCUSE ME!', as if she was stone deaf, or was a foreign exchange student found blocking the exit of the Globe Theatre shortly after the fire alarm had gone off.

Without warning, the milk maid's head twitched violently, making him jump back with a start.

'Good afternoon,' she said, with a warm, seductive smile. 'Would you like to buy some milk?'

'Er, no thank you. I was wondering if you might know where the farm manager is?'

'I'm sorry, I don't know anyone called Farm Manager,' answered the sexy retail-bot. 'Are you sure you wouldn't like to buy some milk?'

'Er, again, thanks but no thanks. The person we're here to see is called Miss Lucy Butterbum?'

'Ah, yes! I know Miss Butterbum. Would you like to have a meeting with her?'

'Yes, please,' said Capstan, feeling as if he was making progress.

'That's nice. I'm sure she'd like to have a meeting with you as well!'

Capstan turned to Dewbush and raised an eyebrow at him. But Dewbush just stared back, seemingly unaware of the subtle but implied sexual reference.

'What time would you like to have a meeting with Miss Butterbum?' continued the retail-bot.

Capstan was tempted to answer, 'Any time, thank you very much!' but if his subordinate was unable to get the joke, it seemed unlikely that the robot would. So instead he just said, 'Could we meet with her now, please?'

'I'm sorry, I didn't recognise that,' said the sexy milk maid, before asking again, 'What time would you like to have a meeting with Miss Butterbum?'

Beside him, Dewbush said, 'You'll need to give her an actual time, sir.'

'Oh! Right, of course,' said Capstan, and stared down at his brand new touch-tech watch that

Dewbush had given him whilst re-entering Earth's atmosphere during their lunch break. But he couldn't for the life of him remember how to make it tell the time, so, turning to Dewbush, for the second time that day asked, 'I don't suppose you know what time it is?'

'Yes, sir. It's sixteen minutes past four, sir.

'Thank you, lieutenant,' said Capstan, before looking back at the sexy retail-bot. 'We'd like to meet Miss Butterbum today, at sixteen minutes past four, please.'

Hearing that, the robot tilted its head to one side, as if deep in thought.

'Trying to get hold of Miss Butterbum for you now,' it said, a moment or two later. 'But you're still able to buy some milk, if you'd like to.'

'Thank you again, but really, I'm fine.'

'Are you sure I can't persuade you to buy some milk?'

'Honestly, I'm fine, but thanks again.'

'It really is very good for you. Just one glass contains nearly all of your daily requirements of calcium, protein, iodine, potassium, phosphorus, vitamins B2 and B12. And not only that, but we can also offer a variety of different types of milk, including skimmed, really-skimmed, semi-skimmed, almost-skimmed, nearly-skimmed, and not-at-all-skimmed.'

'No, really, I'm fine, thank you.'

'How about some yoghurt?' she asked.

'Do you sell yoghurt as well?' asked Capstan. He didn't want yoghurt either, but at least it made a change from being offered milk.

'No, but I'd be happy to order some in for you.'

'Well, I suppose I could…'

Just as Capstan was about to capitulate and place an order for two pints of milk along with a large tub of yoghurt, she held her hand up in front of his face as a clear signal for him to stop talking. She then stared to one side, and started a completely different conversation.

'Good afternoon, Miss Butterbum. I have a man in the shop who would like to have a meeting with you today at sixteen minutes past four.'

There was a pause before she lowered her hand and looked back at Capstan.

'Miss Butterbum would like to know your name and what the meeting would be about?'

'Of course,' said Capstan, and pulled out his brand new Space Police ID, opened it up and held it out for her to see. And as Dewbush did the same thing beside him, Capstan said, 'I'm Detective Inspector Capstan, and this is my colleague, Lieutenant Dewbush. We're here to talk to her about the missing cow.'

The retail-bot examined the two Space Police ID's before raising her hand directly in front of his face again.

'Miss Butterbum. There are actually *two* men here to

see you. One is called Detective Inspector Catspam and the other is Lieutenant Dewbush. They're from the Space Police, and would like to have a meeting with you about the missing cow.'

'Actually, it's pronounced *Capstan*,' interrupted Capstan, but the retail-bot only shoved her hand out even closer to his face so that her palm was almost touching his nose.

'Yes, Miss Butterbum, I'll tell them to wait here for you.'

Lowering her hand, the sexy milk maid looked at both Capstan and Dewbush.

'Miss Butterbum asked for you to wait here. She'll be with you shortly. Meanwhile, I need to give you a copy of this,' and she reached over the counter, pulled a leaflet from out of a clear plastic display unit, and placed it down on the counter in front of them.

'What's this?' asked Capstan.

'It's today's special offer. If you buy more than ten pints of milk from us before we close, you'll get an extra pint for free!'

CHAPTER TWELVE

A FEW MINUTES later, a rather flustered looking young woman wearing large black army boots, khaki green shorts and an untucked blue checked shirt with its sleeves half rolled up, and who, unsurprisingly, had the same colour hair as Dewbush's, just a lot more of it, entered the shop behind them.

'I understand you're looking for me?' she called out with an upbeat tone of voice.

'Miss Butterbum?' asked Capstan, as he turned away from the retail-bot to face the woman, who looked to be in her mid-twenties but could have been closer to a hundred and two for all he knew.

'Unfortunately, yes,' she replied, 'but please God, call me Lucy!'

Capstan smiled at her. Not only was she attractive, in a girl-next-door-to-another-farm sort of a way, but she was the first person he'd met so far who seemed to have anything close to resembling a sense of humour, although now that he thought about it, that was hardly surprising. How could a girl get through life with the surname Butterbum without one? She must have had a hell of a time at school, and if she weren't quite so attractive, he'd almost feel sorry for her.

Pulling out his formal ID, he said, 'Miss, er, Lucy.

I'm Detective Inspector Capstan and this is Lieutenant Dewbush. We're from the UKA Space Police. I understand that you have a cow that's gone missing?'

'Not missing,' she answered. 'Stolen!'

'Ah, I see!' exclaimed Capstan, delighted to have the case elevated up from what he'd thought was going to be nothing more than a larger than average missing pet case to something that was at least criminal in nature.

'And when was the last time you saw the cow?' he asked.

'Oh, I've no idea. The computer logged that only five thousand four hundred and seventy two cows were milked this morning, whereas there should have been five thousand four hundred and seventy three.

'You've got five thousand four hundred and seventy three cows?' He'd not seen a single one when he'd arrived, let alone five thousand four hundred and seventy three of them.

'Er, no. As I just said, we've now only got five thousand four hundred and seventy two. It's happened before, of course, when one died during the night a while back, but when we checked its stall after milking, it simply wasn't there.'

'And where do you keep all these so-called cows?' asked Capstan, thinking that what he considered to be a cow might be radically different from what this lady thought one to be, and that it was probably another electronic device, like an Apple, or a Blackberry, or a

Dyson vacuum cleaner, just one that had been designed to produce milk.

'They're in the cowshed, next door,' she answered, as she wiped her forehead with one of her half rolled up sleeves.

'Well then, I suppose we'd better have a look at where you kept this—cow.'

'Of course. Follow me.'

As she turned to leave, and as Capstan was about to follow on after, the sexy milk maid retail-bot behind them called out, 'Detective Inspector Catspam, you seem to have forgotten your milk!'

'Oh, yes. Sorry. I, er, don't suppose you could keep it here for me, just while I go to the cow shed with Miss Butterbum?'

The robot smiled at him. 'Of course I can. I'll pop it here behind the counter for you, until you get back.'

CHAPTER THIRTEEN

CAPSTAN AND DEWBUSH followed the girl over the sunbaked carpark to what she'd called a cowshed, but which to Capstan looked like an average sized warehouse fronted by two large steel doors locked together with a fair sized padlock.

Lucy Butterbum pulled a tangled mess of keys from her khaki shorts' pocket and stopped at the doors to unlock them.

Behind her, Capstan looked over the exterior of the shed, and asked, 'Is this door always kept locked?'

'Always!' replied Lucy. 'Each cow is worth over $5 million, so we have no choice but to keep them under lock and key.'

'$5 million!' exclaimed Capstan, with initial surprise. But then he remembered that the glass of water that Dewbush had bought him when he'd first woken up had cost $250, so maybe that wasn't so much after all.

'And it's also why we can't afford to have cows go missing,' she added, heaving at one of the now unlocked doors that screeched along on its rollers as the front half of the warehouse began to slowly open.

'You mean, stolen,' corrected Capstan, keen to make sure she hadn't changed her mind, and that it was still a criminal investigation, and not a missing pet type one.

'Sorry, yes, of course.'

In an attempt to see something resembling a real-life cow, or maybe even a miniaturised robotic version of one, Capstan peered inside the dimly lit interior. 'And is there another entrance, other than this?'

'Nope! This is the only way, in *and* out!' answered Lucy, and she led them inside.

As they all walked in through the wide open doorway, and into the relative darkness beyond, a galvanised iron grid rattled underfoot, one that seemed to stretch out over the shed's entire floor. It was only when Capstan stopped to take a look around that he began to hear the echo of an occasional moo, but the cows still sounded as if they were miles away. He could also smell them, confirming at least that they were definitely cows, as no robot on Earth could surely produce such an organic, all-natural pong.

However, despite that, and the fact that his eyes had now adjusted to the relative darkness of the so-called cowshed, for the life of him he still couldn't see any cows. All he could see was warehouse shelving lining the walls, on which were piled dozens of sacks, each with the label YouGet Farm Supplies.

'And you say you have over five thousand cows?' he asked, beginning to run out of places to look for them.

'That's right,' answered Lucy, as she continued over

to the left hand side where there was a large lift housed inside a heavy duty wire-mesh cage.

'Well, I must admit that I'm struggling to see any at all. Are you talking about real cows, or something more pocket-sized?'

'I suppose that depends on how big your pockets are,' she said, turning around to look at his.

Capstan felt himself blush slightly, and was grateful for the cowshed's low light level.

'Forgive me,' she said. 'They're down here,' and with that she flicked a switch on the wall which turned on the shed's lights with a hard electrical snap.

It was only then that Capstan saw the cows.

They were beneath his feet, thousands of them, now clearly visible through the iron grid floor he was standing on, each inside its own cage, and each one on top of another, stacked up like an endless series of shipping crates stretching down into what could easily have been the centre of the Earth. And as if to confirm that they were indeed real-life cows, the one he was standing virtually on top of swivelled its head to fix a deranged eye at him and let out a loud unnerving moo.

'That's Daisy,' said Lucy, with a cheeky smile.

'You mean, you know them all by name?' asked Capstan, still struggling to comprehend the sight before his eyes.

'Only joking,' she answered. 'I call them all Daisy.

Frankly, I can't tell one from another!'

But Dewbush, who up until then had been standing dutifully behind his boss, wasn't at all impressed by her clear violation of the law.

'You do realise, Miss Butterbum,' he started, 'that under Section 57.4 of the Socially Sensible Act 2367, telling a joke in a public place is a criminal offence punishable by up to five years' imprisonment?'

Capstan turned and stared at his subordinate, as if he'd completely lost his mind.

'Gosh! Really?' said Lucy. 'Well, fair enough. It's a fair cop, I suppose,' and held out her hands, ready for them to be cuffed. 'I'll come quietly, but I don't think Daddy will be too pleased.'

'Don't worry, Miss Lucy,' said Capstan, 'the lieutenant here was only joking, weren't you, Dewbush?'

'I can assure you, sir, that I wasn't!' protested Dewbush. 'Section 57.4 of the Socially Sensible Act 2367 clearly states that telling a joke in a public place is a criminal offence punishable by up to five years' imprisonment, sir!'

'All right, all right,' said Capstan, surprised by his lieutenant's enthusiasm. 'I'm sure Miss Lucy didn't mean it.'

'That's not the point, sir. Section 57.4 of the Socially Sensible Act 2367 clearly states that…'

'So you just said, Dewbush!' interrupted Capstan.

'But this isn't a public place though, is it?'

'Isn't it?' asked Dewbush, clearly thrown by the question.

Turning to Miss Butterbum, Capstan asked, 'I don't suppose you'd know if this is classified as a public place?'

'It's a private dairy farm owned by my father, so I'd say that it wasn't.'

'OK, great.' Capstan turned back to face Dewbush. 'So, clearly, no crime has been committed, and we can continue with our investigation, yes?'

'I suppose so, sir, but I think we should at least caution Miss Butterbum. She did clearly tell a joke, sir, and I'm not entirely convinced that just because a building is privately owned means that it's not a public place, especially when the building in question is being used for commercial purposes.'

'I really don't think that will be necessary, Dewbush, but thanks for the suggestion.'

Turning back to Lucy Butterbum, Capstan asked, 'You were going to show us the stall from where your cow was stolen?'

'You can actually see it from here,' she said. 'It's the one nearest the lift, just under the grated floor. The empty one, there,' and to help Capstan identify which one it was out of the hundred or so that made up the upper most level, she pointed at it. 'The thieves must have broken in and simply grabbed the nearest one they could find.'

'And there was definitely a cow there yesterday?'

'As I said, the computer logged that a cow had been milked there, so there must have been. But I didn't see it. The place is fully automated. All I do is keep the food and water supplies stocked up.'

'I see,' said Capstan, and more out of personal curiosity than anything else, asked, 'Don't the cows mind being kept locked in a cage, one on top of the other, miles beneath the ground?'

'I shouldn't have thought so,' she said. 'They're bred to be content standing up in one place for their entire lives, and their water contains a fair amount of Diazepam, which keeps them happy enough. Of course they're naturally stupid as well, which probably helps.'

'So, I suppose it would have been a relatively straight forward process to get the cow into the lift?'

'Yes, but they'd still need to have gained entry into the cowshed first.'

'Was there any sign of a forced entry?' asked Capstan, looking back over at the wide open door.

'None at all.'

Capstan paused for a moment to think, before saying, 'Do you mind if we take another look outside?'

'Be my guest,' and Lucy led them out of the cowshed, back into the scorching heat of Butterbum Farm's carpark, just in time to see a blue and orange delivery truck begin floating down with a YouGet logo on its side, in very much the same way as Capstan and Dewbush must have done just twenty minutes earlier.

As Capstan watched it, fascinated by the technology that allowed it to stay up in the air without any obvious means of doing so, like quadcopter blades or a cable tied to an overhanging tree, an automated voice called out, '*This van is landing. If you are underneath it, please stand clear,*' after which it beeped loudly three times, before the warning was called out again. And when it was about a foot off the ground, the message changed to, '*This vehicle is reversing. If you are behind it, please stand clear,*' as it began to drift backwards, towards the already open warehouse door.

'They're early,' said Lucy, glancing down at her own touch-tech watch, before turning back to Capstan to ask, 'Is there anything more I can help you with?'

'I don't suppose you have any security camera footage?' he asked, as he re-examined the front of the building.

'I'm afraid not. We used to have a security-bot, but it broke down a while back and, to be honest, we never got around to having it fixed.'

'And does anyone else work here, who may have seen something suspicious?'

'There's only Milkmaid Mary, the retail-bot in the shop. You're welcome to have a chat with her but I doubt she'll be of much use. She's very good at selling milk, but unfortunately not much else. Anyway, I'm going to have to have a chat with those delivery guys,' she said, glancing down at her watch again. 'Let me know if you have any news.' With that, she turned and strode over towards the truck which had finished reversing and now had its back end covering the cowshed's entrance.

With Lucy gone, Dewbush asked, 'What should we do now, sir?'

'I'm not sure, Dewbush.'

'It's a shame we couldn't have arrested Miss Butterbum for telling that joke, sir.'

'To be honest, Dewbush, I'm not even sure she did tell a joke.'

'Oh I'm sure she did, sir. She even said that she had. And then at least we'd have had something positive to tell the Chief Inspector.'

'What, that we couldn't find the cow, but instead we were able to arrest the daughter of the guy who owned it?'

'Exactly, sir!'

'C'mon Dewbush. Let's go and have a chat to that milkmaid retail-bot, and see if she did see anything of value.'

'Yes, sir. And you need to pick up that milk you bought as well, sir.'

'Oh yes. I'd almost managed to forget about that,' said Capstan, as they began ambling over to the shop.

'If you don't mind me asking, sir, why did you buy so much milk?'

'I've absolutely no idea, Dewbush. I suppose she was very…persuasive.'

'But she's a retail-bot, sir. They're programmed to be persuasive.'

'Yes, well, I suppose they are.'

'May I suggest, sir, that next time you try saying no? It's one of the first things we're taught at school, sir. If you don't, you'll just end up with a house full of junk.'

'What a brilliant idea, Dewbush. I'd not thought of that!'

'No problem, sir. Any time!'

CHAPTER FOURTEEN

B ACK AT THE WHITE HOUSE at a little after 10am, Gavin Sherburt, President Müller's Chief of Staff, inched open the double doors to the Oval Office and peeked inside.

Relieved to see that President Müller was behind his desk, suited and hopefully booted as he'd promised to be, he proceeded to push his head through the gap, coughing loudly as he did so before saying, 'Excuse me, Mr President. I have Lord Von Splotitty here to see you, along with various members of the press.'

'You mean Tim McTitty Head?' he asked, looking up from the Resolute Desk, the opulent nineteenth-century partners' desk used by so many American presidents before him that had been a gift from Queen Victoria to President Hayes back in 1880, which had since been upgraded to having had the wooden top replaced by a touch-tech screen on which he'd just started playing a game.

'Yes, er, him, Mr President.'

'Well, you'd better bring him in then, unless you'd planned to keep him waiting out there all day?'

'Not at all, Mr President, but should I let Tim McTitty Head—I-I mean, Lord Von Splotitty in first, or should I let the press in to set up?'

'You'd better let Tim McTitty Head in first, Gavin. We should probably have a quiet little tête-à-tête before making our meeting known to the rest of the Galaxy.'

'Very well, Mr President.' Gavin reversed through the gap and proceeded to pull the doors wide open, stepping forward into the Oval Office and announcing a little more formally, 'Mr President, may I introduce the Supreme High Councillor of Titan, and Commander-in-Chief of the Mammary Clans, Lord Von Splotitty.' He stepped to one side and bowed, whilst using his right hand to invite their very special guest inside.

Wobbling into the historic room came what looked almost exactly like a pink blancmange, the only discernible differences being that it was over five feet tall and about seven feet wide, had four eyes, a flattened-out nose, milky-coloured lips, and a giant pair of breasts, and was wearing a purple sarong wrapped around its pudding-shaped moulded middle. And in the place of arms it had a couple of short thick tentacles that were holding on to each other over what might be termed its stomach.

As it weaved and bobbed its way into the room, a giant smile spread all the way out over its top half, as if it was being gouged into by a hungry boy with a larger than average spoon. It bowed, as best it could, as it greeted Müller according to the custom of Titan,

101

saying, 'President Müller. May your mother's milk always flow in your general direction.'

'And yours,' said Müller, as he too bowed with the expected level of reverence.

Unbending himself, Lord Von Splotitty said, 'It is very good of you to take the time to meet with me, President Müller.'

'It is our absolute pleasure, Lord Von Splotitty,' and he stepped around his desk in order to greet his guest. 'And how was the journey?' he asked, holding out a hand which the giant blancmange enveloped in a tentacle, causing Müller to grimace as it slithered over his skin like a horny damp squid.

'It was extremely excellent, President Müller, although I always feel a little uncomfortable having to come down through Earth's atmosphere.'

'And how are you adjusting to our oxygen?'

'I'm always surprised at how quickly we get used to the smell, but we are very fortunate that we can breathe in your air. Anyone would think that we were born to take over your planet!' and another wide smile crept slowly over his face, like a faster than average slug searching for food over a kitchen floor.

'I see your English has improved,' said Müller, a little annoyed that it had, certainly since the last time they'd met.

'As we learn your culture, we also learn your language, and it is now being taught throughout Titan.'

'That is great news! And how are the wife and kids?'

'They continue to grow and drink milk; drink milk and grow. You know what wives and kids are like!' With that, the giant blancmange let out a deep bulbous laugh that sounded like ten tonnes of custard being poured into an empty indoor swimming pool.

'Unfortunately I do,' answered President Müller, who had enough children to populate a small planet.

Returning behind the desk, Müller glanced over at Gavin, who'd closed the doors and was now standing patiently beside them. 'I don't suppose there's anything suitable for our guest to sit on, by any chance?'

'Er…' he replied. He hadn't thought of that, and the two chairs in front of the desk were nowhere near up to the task, even if he'd stuck them together with superglue.

Fortunately for him, Lord Von Splotitty decided to answer the question on his behalf.

'I have no need for a chair, thank you,' the blancmange-shaped creature began. 'As a species we are firm enough to remain in a standing position.'

He didn't look as if he was firm enough to remain in any position, let alone a standing one, and having reached his own chair, Müller said, 'Oh, of course. I remember now. Your species is physically unable to sit down.'

Seeming to take offence, Lord Von Splotitty said, 'We could sit if we wanted to sit, but sitting is not our choice. Unlike you, we are a strong and stable species, and we have no need to bend in half to rest our bodies on something not very comfortable, like a chair.'

'I fully understand,' said Müller, and was about to sit down himself when he thought to ask, 'Do you mind if I do?'

'Of course. But you need to. We don't!' and another wide smile crept over his face.

Sitting down, Müller said, 'I hear you've come to our planet to take part in the Intergalactic Dairy Produce Trade Talks?'

'That's right. But also to meet with Mr Samuel Pollock, your Vice President.'

'And what, may I ask, is it that you are hoping to gain from such discussions?'

Müller already knew the answer, but wondered if his guest would be willing to own up.

Standing a little taller, Lord Von Splotitty said, 'President Müller, before we discovered your species, we were the only planet in the Universe that could produce the milk. At that time we did not know that your planet could also produce the milk. Had someone told us that you could produce the milk, we would not have been so quick to tell you about all the other planets that like to *drink* the milk. And now we find that it is your milk that they want, not ours.'

'And that's our problem, because?'

'I did not say that it was your problem, President

Müller. It is our problem. But it is for us to come up with a solution. And that is why we are here for the trade talks and to have a conversational discussion with your Secretary of State.'

'I see. Well, Pollock's a good man, and I'm sure that he'll be able to help you in any way that he can. Tell me, what sort of thing did you have in mind?'

'We wish to talk with him how we can get something in return for having told you about the other planets that like to drink the milk, to help us with…how do I say…compensituate us for not making as much money as we did before we discovered you.'

'You mean to, help *compensate* you,' corrected Müller.

'That is what I said.'

'It wasn't, but that aside, as I said, I'm sure he'd be delighted to help in any way that he can. And I'm sure that together, the three of us will be able to agree on a suitably generous figure to help *compensate* you for your financial losses, as well as to give you an extra little something for having been so kind as to have gone out of your way to discover us, and for then introducing us to all the other life forms with which we now do so much business.'

'You are happy to do that?' asked Lord Von Splotitty, clearly surprised. He'd been expecting considerably more political opposition to his proposal.

'I'll go so far as to promise that we will!' said Müller. 'After all, if you hadn't discovered us, we'd never have become a planet with one of the largest GDPs in the known Universe.'

'That is very kind of you, President Müller. Very kind. Indeed it is.'

'Now, unfortunately, I have some really boring work to be getting on with, but my Chief of Staff, Gavin here, will be able to look after you for the rest of the day. Hopefully I'll then be able to join you for dinner, later on this evening.'

Stepping forward from the back of the room, Gavin said, 'Do you think we could now invite the press in, Mr President?'

'Of course, the press. I'd nearly managed to forget about them. Do you mind, Lord Von Splotitty, if we let the media in to take some pictures and maybe ask a few questions?'

'I would be happy with that,' the giant blancmange-type creature replied.

As Gavin re-opened the double doors, a gaggle of reporters began falling over themselves, jostling for a prime position within the Oval Office as they all started taking a seemingly endless number of touch-tech photographs along with video footage whilst calling out a series of pointless and predominantly stupid questions, most of which related to how long it had taken Lord Von Splotitty to travel from Titan to

Earth, if it was true that his species weren't able to sit down, and if they couldn't, how then did they go to the toilet. And as they did that, Gavin took up his position to the side and slightly behind his boss.

When President Müller felt his guest was suitably distracted, he whispered to Gavin, 'When you see Pollock, make sure you tell him to agree to whatever it is that this Tim McTitty Head wants.'

'Yes, Mr President.'

As the press moved on to asking if everyone on Titan looked like a dessert made of milk, cream and sugar, all set in a mould and served cold, Gavin took the opportunity to ask, 'Did you really mean all that stuff about giving them compensation, Mr President?'

'Of course not, you idiot. And don't forget to make sure he gets really drunk at dinner, is introduced to our very best in-house prostitutes, and that he's left alone with them whilst being filmed. Understood?'

'Yes, Mr President. Fully understood, Mr President.'

CHAPTER FIFTEEN

THE FOLLOWING DAY, Capstan awoke to the sound of the soft warm undulations of a woman's voice.

'Good morning, Andrew,' it said, sounding like a hypnotherapist saying hello to a regular client. 'It's half past seven in the morning. Would you like to get up now?'

At first he'd no idea where the voice had come from or, more worryingly, where he actually was. But after a moment or two the memories of the previous day came flooding back.

So much had happened since he'd come out of his coma that he just lay there for a few minutes in the strange bed, looking around the still unfamiliar environment of his new private quarters that were lit by a dim blue light coming from the toilet seat. As he did so, he suddenly began to feel home sick. He'd never thought it possible, but he was missing his wife. He was used to waking up next to her, and not doing so left him feeling vulnerable and insecure; and now that he was thinking about her, his mind naturally turned to his children, who must have passed away many decades earlier.

As he lay there he found himself reminiscing about

other parts of his old life as well, his semi-detached house for example, also his car, and even his old job, although that did seem to be remarkably similar to his new one.

Staring around the very compact room that only had a toilet in one corner, a shower in the other, a table with an attached seat in the middle, and a YouGet magical shopping facility built into the wall opposite his bed, he found himself missing almost everything about his old life, even his former subordinate, Simon Peter Dewbush, as opposed to his new one, Peter Simon Dewbush. In fact, the only thing he wasn't missing was his leg. The new one he now had was better in every way, and he reached down to make sure it was still there. It was, which also confirmed that the previous day's events hadn't been some sort of weird surreal dream, and that he was in his new home, the one that Lieutenant Dewbush had been kind enough to take him to when they'd arrived back the previous day from their trip to his former home, the now scorched land he'd always known as England, but which wasn't anymore. It wasn't even Great Britain, but now had the God-awful title of the United Kingdom of America, and seemed to be different in every way from the place he'd once called home. The only thing he could think of that *was* the same was that they still spoke English, with an English accent, and not some mid-western American drawl that he'd have thought likely, given the fact that they'd been taken over by their American cousins several hundred years earlier.

Momentarily, his mind drifted back to thinking about his wife and children again, but doing so only made his bottom lip quiver and brought tears to his eyes. Wiping them away he decided, there and then, that at some point he'd look to see if he could find out what had happened to them, and if he had any relatives living today who he could maybe pop in and have a cup of tea with.

Having made up his mind to do that, he turned his attention back to the case he was working on, that of the missing cow, the one that hopefully had been stolen, and hadn't simply effected an escape from what had seemed more like a prison for psychotic four-legged bovine criminals than a dairy farm.

Climbing out of bed he took his pyjamas off and headed over to the shower cubicle. Compared to many things in the 25th Century, it was easy enough to use. He just had to step inside and it turned itself on automatically, and at the perfect temperature as well.

As he washed himself with a very normal looking bar of soap, he let his mind ruminate on the events of the following day, starting off at Butterbum Farm.

After Miss Butterbum had headed off to see to her delivery, he'd led Dewbush back into the shop to speak with the retail-bot Lucy had called Milk Maid

Mary. But she'd been about as much use to the investigation as Lucy had said she would be, and instead of helping them with their inquiries had simply done her very best to sell Capstan some more milk, on top of the eleven pints he'd already bought from her.

It was when they'd come out of the shop that he'd noticed the YouGet delivery van had gone and that Lucy was nowhere to be seen, even though the cowshed door was still wide open. But as he'd not been able to think of anything else to ask her, it hardly mattered, and they'd made their way back to their car where Dewbush had helped him to load his shopping. Their unmarked space police car had no boot, or trunk as Dewbush had referred to it, so they'd loaded the milk onto the backseats which, unlike the boot, was necessary for the transportation of arrested members of the public under suspicion of doing something illegal, like cow theft, or murder, or worse still, according to Dewbush at least, telling a joke with the illicit intent of making someone laugh.

Once Capstan's eleven pints of milk had been secured using the seatbelts, they'd begun the journey back to the police space station, during which time Dewbush had helped Capstan to draft up an interim report. Fortunately, it hadn't taken them long, and with Dewbush's help, Capstan was able to email the finished version over to Chief Inspector Chapwick before they'd arrived safely back on board the UKA

Police Space Station 999.

There, Dewbush had very kindly shown Capstan to his living quarters, given him a very quick tour of how everything worked, including the shower, toilet and the YouGet hole in the wall shopping device which every cabin seemed to have, and had left Capstan to spend an exhausting hour trying to order a cottage pie for his supper, which he'd eventually managed to do. However, in the process he'd also been persuaded to buy some French fries, a strawberry milkshake, a pair of chrome-plated candlestick holders, a matching set of picture frames, ten plastic flower pots, a picnic basket, and everything else you could possibly need for a romantic outdoor lunch for two back on earth, including a rug, two wide-brimmed hats, insect repellent, and two bottles of sun lotion, each with an SPF of two hundred and ninety five.

As he stepped out of the shower, he noticed a device mounted to the wall besides his door had started to play a funky sort of a tune as it glowed blue. Thinking that it must have been some sort of a phone device, possibly the landline, he wrapped a towel around his middle and padded over the warm soft flooring to see if he could work out how to answer it. And to his surprise, he did.

'Good morning, sir, it's Lieutenant Dewbush.'

'Good morning, Dewbush. And how are you today?'

'Very well, thank you, sir. Did you sleep well?'

'Remarkably well, thank you.'

'I don't suppose you're nearly ready, sir? It's just that the Chief Inspector's been on the phone and he wants to see us straight away.'

'Did he say what it's about?'

'No, sir. He just asked me to come round and pick you up.'

'OK. Where are you now?'

'Standing outside your door, sir.'

'Oh, right! Well, let me get dressed, and I'll be right with you.'

CHAPTER SIXTEEN

ABOUT FIFTEEN MINUTES later, Capstan and Dewbush were shown in to Chief Inspector Chapwick's office, with all its polished white walls and invisible furniture.

Glancing up from his desk, Chapwick said, 'Come in, you two and please, take a seat,' before returning to look as if he was staring at his trousers, in much the same way as he'd been doing the previous day.

As Dewbush stepped forward, Capstan hesitated. Even though he'd done it before, the idea of having to sit on something he couldn't actually see still made him feel uneasy. But then he saw what must be called the seat's landing lights, or something similar, looking as if they were floating in mid-air, and headed over towards them. Making sure that he was lined up between the two, with the red one on his left and the green to his right, he eased himself down as Dewbush had already done beside him.

Looking up again, Chapwick smiled at them both and to Capstan asked, 'How are you settling in?'

'All right, I suppose, all things considered, sir.'

'And what did you make of Port's Mouth yesterday?'

'A little on the warm side, sir.'

114

'Really?' he said, and looking over at Dewbush, asked, 'I thought the forecast was for it to be rather cold for the time of year?'

'Er, Dewbush did say that, yes, sir. But it's just that it used to be quite a lot colder back in my time.'

'I'd no idea! Anyway, I received your interim report on the missing cow case,' he said, looking back down at his trousers. 'It's a little on the short side, isn't it?'

'Sorry, but what is, sir?'

'Your report, Capstan.'

'Do you think so, sir?'

'Well, a little, yes. All it says is that you spoke to Miss Butterbum who said that the cow hadn't gone missing but that it had been stolen instead, and that she hadn't seen who'd done it, so you came back to the station.'

'Forgive me, sir,' said Capstan, 'but I thought I'd written a little more than that.'

Chapwick looked up at him and raised an eyebrow. 'Not much more, Capstan. I'll read it to you, shall I?' and without waiting for a response, began to do so. 'We spoke to Miss Butterbum who said that the cow hadn't gone missing but it had been stolen instead, and that she hadn't seen who'd done it, so we decided to come straight back to the station.'

'That sounds more like it, sir,' said Capstan. 'Although we did also speak to a retail-bot girl thing in the farm's shop as well, sir, but she wasn't much use to be honest.'

'I see. And that was normal, back in the 21st Century, was it?'

'What, to interview a retail-bot girl thing as part of an on-going criminal investigation?' asked Capstan, momentarily confused.

'Er, no, Capstan. For police reports to be quite so concise?'

'Oh. Well, I'd say that it probably was normal for interim reports to be on the short side, yes, sir, but the final ones would generally be a little longer.'

'Well, I suppose that's fair enough, but in this day and age, Capstan, you're expected to include a lot more information, even for an interim report, like where you went, for example, and the time of arrival, as well as full details of who you interviewed, what they said, an accurate description of what had taken place, and a brief summary, including your own observations and the recommended next steps.'

'Yes, sir. I'll make sure we do that next time, sir.'

'Well, as I said, I guess we do things a little differently now. Anyway, that wasn't what I wanted to talk to you about. There's been a new *development*.'

'On the stolen cow case, sir?' asked Capstan, hoping there'd been a lead of some sort, because without one he had no idea what to do next.

'Miss Butterbum appears to have gone missing, as well as the cow.'

'Oh dear. I'm sorry to hear that, sir. But just to be clear, the cow hasn't gone missing, sir, it has been stolen, as stated in my report, sir.'

'What? Oh yes, stolen, of course. Anyway, we don't normally give as much priority to missing persons as we do to missing—I mean stolen cows, simply because cows are worth a lot more than humans. However, as this is the daughter of Sir Percy Butterbum, who probably owns half the cows in the UKA, we're giving this top priority. And as you're already investigating the case of the cow, I thought you may as well investigate the case of the girl whilst you're at it.'

'Yes, sir,' said Capstan, with unusual enthusiasm. He'd taken a liking to Lucy, and so was quite happy to have a bit of a look around for her.

'Fortunately,' continued Chapwick, 'she shouldn't be too difficult to find, as her father has had her implanted with a tracking device.'

'A tracking device, sir?'

'That's right, Capstan. It's a clever little invention that helps us to locate things that go missing.'

'Sorry, sir, but I actually knew that. We had them in our time as well, but we only used them on cars, not people, sir, unless of course they were criminals out on probation.'

'Well, yes, I suppose it's unusual even in this day and age to put a tracking device on a person, but I'm given the impression that Sir Percy is quite protective of his daughter, and likes to know where she is at all times. But it's to our advantage now, although there's a bit of a snag.'

'A snag, sir?'

'It only works up to a distance of 240,000 miles, and as of last night, it went out of range.'

'Sorry, sir, but did you say that it only works up to a distance of 240,000 miles, and as of last night, it went out of range?' repeated Capstan, as his brain attempted to comprehend what the Chief Inspector had just told him.

'That's right. Basically, it can track people to the moon, but doesn't go much beyond that.'

'So you're saying that Lucy, I-I mean, Miss Butterbum has a tracker on her which says that she's currently 240,000 miles away from Earth?'

'Beyond that now, I'm afraid, yes. I'll send you over her last known co-ordinates, but the computer's plotted her trajectory and she's apparently on her way to Titan. So I suggest you make your way over in that general direction, and hopefully you'll be able to pick up the signal again at some point.'

'You want us to go to Titan?' asked Capstan, now staring at the Chief Inspector as if he'd just begun to grow an extra head.

'Oh, sorry. I keep forgetting that space travel must still be a bit of a novelty for you.'

'B-but isn't Titan another planet, sir?' asked

Capstan.

'It's actually one of Saturn's moons, about 87 million miles away from Earth, which isn't as far as it sounds. Once you're up to light speed it should only take you about an hour or so.'

'An hour or so?' repeated Capstan.

'Travelling at 671 million miles per hour, I'd say that's about right, wouldn't you, Dewbush?'

'It will take us 50 minutes, sir,' answered the lieutenant. 'Once we've reached light speed, but unfortunately our car only does 0 to 671 million miles in 120 minutes, sir, and it will take us just as long to slow down.'

'OK, well, about five hours then. So if you leave now, you should be there in time for lunch, just about,' he said, glancing down at his watch.

CHAPTER SEVENTEEN

LUCY BUTTERBUM, daughter of Sir Percy Butterbum, the owner of the Butterbum dairy farm franchise and subsequently one of the richest men in the UKA, was having a disturbing dream. She was dreaming that she was lying on a bed of straw and that her face was being licked by a cow. But the dream quickly became even more disturbing when she realised it wasn't a dream at all; she was indeed lying on a bed of straw with her face being licked by a cow, and one that was standing directly over her as it did.

'*Ewwwe…yuk!*' she said, wiping her face with her arms as she scrambled out from underneath it.

'Ah! You're awake. Finally!' said an almost good-looking young man sitting opposite her with beige skin, sandy hair, and a matching-coloured beard, and wearing an orange and blue YouGet delivery man's uniform.

'Where the hell am I?' she demanded, as she stood up, staring around at first the cow and then the young man, feeling completely disorientated.

'You're in the back of a YouGet delivery truck, about halfway between Earth and Titan,' said the man.

She only heard the first bit, about being in the YouGet delivery truck, and as the memory of what

120

had happened at the farm began to come back to her, she said, 'You're that YouGet guy, delivering farm supplies?'

'Sort of.'

'But you weren't delivering farm supplies, were you? You were stealing one of our cows!'

'We were liberating one of them, yes. In fact, it was the one that's behind you, and she's off to join the other one we took the day before yesterday.'

'And I suppose you've kidnapped me in the hope that my father will pay you a large amount of money for my safe return?'

'Er, no, sorry. Why? Did you want to be kidnapped?'

'Of course I didn't want to be kidnapped!'

'Well, that's all right then,' and he smiled at her before looking at the cow.

'I'm sorry, but what do you mean, "That's all right then"?'

'Look, miss, you haven't been kidnapped. You just got in the way when we were taking the cow. So if you take a seat, we'll drop you off when we get there and you'll be able to make your way home.'

'I think I'd rather get out now, if it's all the same to you,' she said.

'You want to get out now?' he asked, staring at her.

'Yes, please. I need to get back to work, so if you'd be so kind,' and she looked around her for a door, perhaps one which had "EXIT" written on it.

'But—we're half way to Titan, travelling at 671 million miles an hour. I'm not sure what would happen to you if you did step out now, but I don't think it would make suitable viewing for children.'

'We're halfway to Titan!' she exclaimed.

'As I said—Titan. You know, it's the moon that goes around Saturn.'

'I'm sorry, but who did you say you were again?' she asked.

With a proud grin, he held out his hand, saying, 'I'm Starstrider,' by way of formal introduction.

Ignoring the proffered hand, she said, 'Really?'

'The one and only!'

'And Starstrider's your real name?'

'That's right!'

'Honestly?'

'Well, no. But that's what everyone calls me.'

'And what do you do when you're not out stealing cows and kidnapping women? Force children to give you their dinner money on their way to school?'

'As I said, miss, we *haven't* stolen the cow and we *haven't* kidnapped you. We're Intergalactic Free Rangers!'

'Intergalactic Free Rangers?' she asked. 'And what do they do? Travel around the galaxy laying eggs?'

'Er, no, we don't, *actually!* Our mission is to free animals from the cruel oppressive practices of modern day intensive farming methods.'

'So, you *are* cow thieves, then?'

'Not at all! We release them on Titan where they're considered to be sacred animals, and where they're allowed to roam free, not locked in a cage miles beneath the ground being endlessly milked for the sole financial benefit of Sir Percy Butterbum!'

'And not forgetting the odd one or two people spread throughout the galaxy who're partial to a spot of milk in their tea.'

'That's not the point! In the olden days, cows were allowed to roam free, on a field of lush green grass, and were only milked once a day. They weren't kept locked up in cages, one stacked on top of the other, miles beneath the ground.'

'You do realise that I'm Sir Percy Butterbum's daughter, don't you?' she asked, as she put her hands on her hips and gave him a defiant look.

The young man stared up at her. 'You are?' he asked, clearly a little taken aback by the news.

'Yes, I am! And I can assure you that he's going to be none too pleased when he finds out that I'm not at work, where I'm supposed to be, but instead have been kidnapped by a bunch of egg-laying animal rights activists. So I suggest that you turn this thing around immediately before he calls the police and has you lined up against a wall and shot!'

'Ok, look, we didn't know you were his daughter,

but we can't turn around now, I'm afraid. Not when we're travelling at light speed. You'll just have to wait till we get to Titan, and then catch the next shuttle back.'

She folded her arms and glowered at him.

'Honestly, miss, there's nothing I can do about it. Any attempt to alter course going this fast and we'd be vaporised before Daisy here could say "Moo".' So I suggest you take a seat and relax. We should be there in a few hours,' and as he too folded his arms, he looked at the cow before muttering to himself, 'although we'd have been there about a day ago if this stupid delivery truck wasn't so slow.'

Lucy stood there and considered her options for a moment. Unfortunately the man was right. She was going to have to stick it out. But when she got to Titan she was damned if she was going to leave without her cows, and would have to work out a way of getting them back to Earth with her. So as she thought about how she was going to do that, she plonked herself down beside the so-called Intergalactic Free Ranger and joined him in staring at the cow, which just stared back at them, seemingly oblivious to the fact that it had been liberated from its former cruel life of intensive industrialised farming and was to be released to roam free on Titan, in just a few short hours' time.

CHAPTER EIGHTEEN

A S PRESIDENT DICK Müller stood outside what had been Lord Von Splotitty's room for the night, which was the Lincoln Bedroom suite, located in the southeast corner of the White House, and which just happened to have an impressive one-way mirror facing its presidential-sized bed behind which he'd had installed a film production studio, complete with a camera, sound recording equipment and a touch-tech video editing desk, he was feeling like it was Christmas morning.

He was right in one respect. It was morning. Twenty-five minutes past nine, to be exact. But it wasn't Christmas. It just happened to feel like it, and that was because, about half an hour earlier, his Chief of Staff, Gavin Sherburt, had been kind enough to give him a present. It wasn't much of a present, but it was something he'd been wanting ever since the first time he'd received an old fashioned postcard from his current very special guest, Lord Von Splotitty, on Intergalactic Earth Found Day. That was the day Earth had officially been discovered by the Mammary Clans of Titan, and on that day, every year since, he'd received the very same postcard on the back of which simply said, "You're Welcome!"

125

After decades of the humiliation of having been "discovered", and being reminded of the fact every single year by means of a postcard, the day had finally arrived for President Müller's retribution.

Having spent years attempting to lure Splotitty to visit the White House, without making it too obvious that he actually wanted him to come anywhere near the place, Dick Müller now had in his possession what he'd been trying to get hold of all that time. And having had a quick scan through it on double speed, he was supremely confident that it would do the trick.

Taking a breath to help calm his over-excited nerves, he knocked on the Lincoln Bedroom suite's door and called out, 'ROOM SERVICE,' doing his best to sound like a girl. Then he just waited there patiently as he lifted himself up and down on the balls of his feet whilst staring up at the ceiling.

It wasn't long before the door was opened, and by none other than Lord Von Splotitty himself, looking considerably more saggy than he'd done the previous day; less like a perfectly set pink blancmange and more like Bagpuss after being accidentally trodden on.

'President Müller!' Splotitty exclaimed, somewhat surprised to see the President of Earth standing there, when he'd been expecting a sexy housemaid-bot.

'Hello, Timmy!' said Müller, with a huge smile, and barged straight past him. And as he made his way straight through to the bedroom, he called back,

'How'd you sleep last night?'

'Oh, er…' began Splotitty, before manoeuvring himself around to begin wobbling after him, as quickly as he possibly could.

Entering the historic bedroom, and after quickly saying hello to the three naked human female prostitutes, one of whom was wearing a latex rubber cow mask, who were just waking up in the presidential-sized bed, he turned to stare at the mirror opposite and grinned at his own reflection.

When Splotitty was finally able to waddle his way through to the bedroom, in a conversational tone President Müller asked, 'Did you know that this room used to be Abraham Lincoln's office?'

'Er…?' replied Lord Von Splotitty, who'd never heard of anyone called Abraham Lincoln before, and was still trying to work out why President Müller had called him Timmy, and why he'd then pushed his way in to what he thought was his private room, without even having had the decency to ask before doing so.

'And it was in 1825,' continued Müller, as he stretched out his arms and began searching around behind the mirror's ornate gold frame, 'that he had it converted. And it was right here, in 1863, that he signed the Emancipation Proclamation which effectively brought an end to that barbaric period of human history known as Slavery.'

Finding the hidden button he'd been looking for,

Müller pushed it, and took a step back to watch the giant mirror begin to slowly lift up towards the ornately decorated high ceiling. 'And it's thought that he used this as his office right up to the time when he was assassinated, just two years later, in April 1865. But that does of course beg the question why it's called Lincoln's Bedroom, and not Lincoln's Office. Anyway,' he turned to look behind him, which was where Lord Von Splotitty was now standing, staring at what was gradually being revealed to him behind the mirror, with his mouth hanging open like an empty pillow case waiting to be stuffed with a pillow, 'I'd like to introduce you to Lincoln's Bedroom Film Production Unit. On the far left is our cameraman, Phil Campbell. Next to him is the audio engineer, Joseph Ward. Then there's Jake Price, the production manager, Lance Phillips, the producer, and last but by no means least, the film director, Maurice Patterson.'

As he introduced each of the people sitting behind the touch-tech video editing desk, they waved first at Lord Von Splotitty and then at the three prostitutes, who giggled, clearly a little embarrassed, and waved back.

Reaching into his pocket, President Müller pulled out what looked like a normal memory stick.

'And I have here an edited version of what was recorded last night, which I'm sure you'll find to be quite…stimulating,' and pointing the memory stick at a bare wall to their right, he pressed a button on it which triggered a built-in film projection unit to start playing its contents. As the three girls sat up in bed to start watching themselves on the wall, where they'd begun cavorting and gyrating their nubile young bodies on top of Lord Von Splotitty, as if he was a cross between a water bed and an indoor bouncy castle, they watched as the one wearing the rubber cow mask started pouring cream onto one particular part of his rather peculiar shaped anatomy whilst saying 'Moo' rather loudly. And as she did that, the other two began taking it in turns to lick it off.

'This is great!' said President Müller. 'Would anyone like popcorn?'

As the three girls and the five members of the film production crew all put their hands up for popcorn, Lord Von Splotitty's entire pudding-like body began to tremble all over, as if someone had tied him to a go-kart and pushed him headfirst down the Lincoln Memorial steps.

'Now, if you'd like to step next door, I'd be happy to discuss the terms of your surrender.'

'The t-t-terms of my what?' asked Splotitty.

'Your surrender. You know, it's what you do when you've been caught on film having cream being licked off you by two human female prostitutes whilst another one, who it would appear is wearing some sort of a rubber cow mask, is saying, "Moo".

'B-b-but…what am I supposed to *surrender?*'

'Titan of course! And if you could do so just as soon as you get back, I'd be very grateful. But should you decide that you'd rather not hand over Titan to Earth, as requested, then I'd be more than happy to send the full version of this video, which would appear to be almost educational in content, over to the Intergalactic News Federation in exchange for a large amount of money. I'm sure they'd be more than happy to include it in tomorrow's broadcast. In fact, it's so good they'd probably want to use it as part of their title sequence for the next six months or so.'

CHAPTER NINETEEN

AFTER A QUICK and easy descent down through Titan's relatively thin atmosphere, compared to Earth's at any rate, the YouGet delivery truck landed in a parking area in the centre of a pretty little cul-de-sac surrounded by pink pudding-shaped semi-detached houses on the outskirts of Titania, Titan's capital city.

Starstrider stood up and stretched his arms up above his head, and after a lengthy yawn, said to Lucy, 'We must be here.'

Lucy got up, and immediately felt as if she'd lost weight, a lot of weight in fact; and as she found herself almost bouncing her way over to see how the cow was doing after her rather long eighty-seven million mile trip to Titan, she wondered if the new low-fat cottage cheese diet she'd been on for the last three weeks had finally begun to pay off.

As she began stroking the cow, who seemed happy enough, Starstrider took a couple of heavy-looking black coats down from some hooks on the side of the van, along with what resembled two bright red motorcycle crash helmets, and handed one of each to Lucy. 'Here. You'll need these.'

Taking both from him, she asked, 'What are they

for?'

Starstrider rolled his eyes. 'Have you never been to Titan before?'

'Funnily enough, not recently, no,' Lucy replied, 'but only because, up until today, nobody's been kind enough to force me into the back of a YouGet delivery truck and drag me all the way here without even having the basic decency to ask if I wanted to come!'

Ignoring her, Starstrider said, 'Well, Titan's a lot colder than what you're used to, and the gravity here is only about fourteen percent of Earth's. The coat you've got has weights sewn into a solar heated lining, so it will help to weigh you down as well as to keep you warm. And although the Mammary Clans are lucky to be able to breathe on Earth, the atmosphere here is almost entirely methane gas, which is what cows produce naturally, when they…when they…you know.'

Lucy nodded, to let him know that she knew what he was thinking of but was clearly too embarrassed to say it out loud.

'It's another reason why bovines are considered to be sacred here. Not only do they produce full cream milk, but the Mammary Clans can actually breathe their farts!'

Realising he'd just said the word out loud, Starstrider went a little pink around the edges.

'So anyway,' he continued, as quickly as he could,

132

'the only milk-producing species they have here is the Dampfnudel, but they only make what is effectively skimmed milk, it doesn't contain any cream, and they produce nitrous oxide when they…you know, which not even the Mammary Clans can breathe.'

'And so what's the helmet for?' asked Lucy. He had an impressive knowledge of milk-producing species, from both Earth and Titan, but he clearly had a problem with being able to stay on subject.

'Oh, sorry. I was just saying that there's no oxygen here, just methane gas. The helmet has a built-in oxygen supply, so you'll need it to breathe.'

'Got it,' said Lucy, and as she put the oxygen helmet down onto the bench she'd been sitting on in order to begin to fight her way into the heavy coat, she asked, 'What about Daisy?'

'Who?'

'The cow! Remember?'

'Oh yes, Daisy. Of course! Same for her, I'm afraid,' and he ducked under the cow's head to the other side of the van, from where he threw a thick blanket over her back. 'You see those weights down there?' he said, pointing at what looked to be a pile of bricks. 'If you could put one into each of the pockets you'll find along the edges of the blanket, I'll try to put her oxygen mask on.'

When all three of them were suitably attired, Starstrider squeezed himself between the cow and

Lucy to get to the back of the truck. There he pulled one of two levers down and watched as a pressure gauge alongside it dropped until a light underneath it turned from red to green. He then pulled the other lever down and stared up as the very top of the truck's back section began to fall towards the road below, where Lucy could just about make out two people standing on the pavement beyond, both wearing the same black coats and red crash helmets; but the natural light outside was so dim, they could just as easily be bollards, or sign posts, or even street lights that had yet to be turned on.

'You've already met Oberon and Calisto,' said Starstrider. The two people waved up at Lucy. 'Oberon does accounts and marketing, whilst Calisto deals with driving and navigation.'

With the formal introductions made, Oberon and Calisto marched up the truck's door that now acted as a gangplank, and together the four of them worked to turn Daisy the cow around, inside the truck, before leading her down the ramp onto the pavement below.

'What happens to Daisy now?' asked Lucy, gazing up in awe at the planet Saturn which filled up virtually the entire sky above her, and whose rings glowed bright in the surrounding twilight, so close that she felt as if she could almost reach out and touch them.

As the three men worked together to close the back of the truck, Starstrider said, 'We'll show you.' He then grasped the side of Daisy the cow's oxygen mask and began leading her towards the side gate of one of the domed shaped semi-detached houses.

At the rear of the house, they stepped out into an average-sized suburban garden with bright green grass that was clearly artificial, and which was surrounded by a wooden fence. In the middle stood another cow, wearing the same weighted-down blanket and oxygen mask, trying to eat the grass, but unable to do so because of its breathing apparatus.

'That's the cow we liberated the other day,' Starstrider said. 'We call her Mary,' and as if she'd heard her name, the cow lifted her head to watch them approach.

'You've only got two cows?' asked Lucy. For some reason she'd been expecting to see an entire heard, roaming free over rolling hills of lush green grass as far as the eye could see, not just one stuck in someone's back garden.

'Well, we've only just started. Oberon and Calisto are going to put up a sign later on at the front of the house announcing the opening of Titan's very first Bovine Zoo. We'll see how much interest that can generate. But our big plan is to buy some land and build a large greenhouse that we can keep oxygenated and grow real grass. Then we're going to get some more cows and launch a Titan-wide advertising campaign. And if we can teach the cows to do a few tricks, we might start a travelling circus as well!'

'So you *are* planning on making a profit from it then!' asked Lucy, in an accusatory tone. She'd always suspected that there must have been some sort of financial angle to their rather ambitious, not to say highly illegal little venture.

'Yes, but only to make enough money to pay our expenses. It's not cheap, you know, travelling back and forth between here and Earth, and you can see how happy Mary is. That's all that matters, at the end of the day,' and they all gazed over at the incumbent cow, which went back to trying to eat the grass. 'And they'll be even happier when they can graze freely without the need for the oxygen mask.'

As Lucy watched the cow take a step forward, as it tried its luck with another section of the artificial lawn it was walking on, she was beginning to see what Starstrider had been going on about. The picture before her, of a cow moving freely about on what at least looked like grass, had an uplifting, almost spiritual feel to it; and underneath the blanket and oxygen mask she even thought the cow did look as if it was happy.

'So, anyway, sorry for kidnapping you, and everything,' apologised Starstrider. 'Would you like to have a look around Titan before you go, or are you keen to get straight home?'

Looking back up at the spectacular view of Saturn again she said, 'I suppose it's not every day I get to go to Titan. Perhaps I could spend the day in Titania, and have a look around?'

'Sure thing! Although a day may be a little too long. In Earth time each one lasts for fifteen days, twenty-two hours, and forty-one minutes.'

'I suppose jet lag must be a problem then?'

'I can't say I've stayed long enough to find out.'

Feeling less like going home by the minute, Lucy asked, 'Is there anything to do in town?'

'A fair bit,' replied Starstrider, as he led her back around the side of the house. 'The Mammary Clans are surprisingly cultured, considering they all look like moulded shaped puddings. They have a few restaurants, most of which are milk-themed, and they've even got a cinema which I went to once. But the film they were showing was rubbish. I didn't have a clue what was going on and they didn't even bother to give it subtitles, and when I found out it went on for two and a half days, I walked out.'

Realising he'd been talking too much, as he had a habit of doing when in the company of attractive young women, which wasn't very often, he said, 'Anyway, I'll give you the tour myself, if you like?'

CHAPTER TWENTY

ALTHOUGH THEIR unmarked UKA Space Police car wasn't all that fast, compared to some privately owned space vehicles, it could travel about ten times the speed of your average delivery truck, especially building up to and decelerating from light speed. So it didn't take Capstan and Dewbush long to catch up to Lucy and the gang of Intergalactic Free Rangers. And thanks to the tracking device that Lucy's father had had embedded into her leg when she was born, which she'd yet to discover, they were able to land just a few feet away from the YouGet truck that was still parked outside the quiet semi-detached house in a small cul-de-sac on the outskirts of Titania.

'Any sign of her?' asked Capstan, trying to keep his mind off the fact that he'd just landed on one of Saturn's moons having spent the last five hours travelling a distance of eighty-seven million miles at an average speed of 670 million miles per hour.

'No, nothing, sir. Just the back of an empty truck.'

'How about the cow?'

'I can't see a cow, sir, but they're normally kept underground.'

'OK, well, the tracker says Lucy's here somewhere, so we'd better wait for her to show up.'

'Hold on, sir, but isn't that the same truck that was parked outside Butterbum Dairy Farm yesterday, sir?'

'You know what, Dewbush, I think you could be right!' exclaimed Capstan. 'And judging by the straw inside it, not to mention what looks like cow poo, it looks as if they had a cow in the back of it! That Lucy Butterbum girl *must* be involved, somehow.' Looking over his shoulder, he asked, 'Can you reverse this up a bit? There's another car there you can park behind, and that way we won't stick out like a sore thumb.'

'OK. So, I'll reverse-park then, shall I, sir?'

'Yes please, Dewbush.'

'Right you are,' and Dewbush shunted it into reverse and carefully backed it in behind the other car.

'How was that, sir?' he asked with a triumphant look, clearly hoping to have impressed his new boss with his reverse-parking skills.

'Very good, Dewbush.'

'Did you used to do this a lot, sir?'

'What, reverse-park?'

'No, sir. Be on a stakeout?'

'Oh, yes. Quite a lot, I suppose, although I've never been staked-out behind a YouGet space delivery truck on one of Saturn's moons before. But I do seem to remember finding myself parked outside a number of YouGet shops, back in the day,' and he gazed off into the distance as he remembered those times in Portsmouth, so many hundreds of years before, but which for him still felt like only about three weeks ago.

'Did YouGet have shops back then, sir?'

'They certainly did, Dewbush!'

'What were they like, sir? I mean, did you actually go inside them and buy stuff from a really large hole in the wall?'

'Sort of. But back then we didn't have your clever hole in the wall thing. Not for shopping, at least.'

'How did you buy stuff from them then, sir?'

'Well, first you'd go into the shop and look through a laminated catalogue. You'd then pick out what you'd want, and write the item's code number on a bit of paper with a wooden pencil they use to provide. Then you'd take that paper to the cashier - that was where you'd pay for it. They'd then give you a receipt and you were told to go to a certain collection point whilst they dug out your item from the warehouse at the back. After about five minutes they'd eventually bring out what you'd bought, and after signing your receipt, you'd be able to carry the item home to do whatever it was that you wanted to do with it.'

There was a pause in the conversation as Dewbush attempted to understand the old fashioned YouGet sales process that this man from Earth's distant past had explained to him, but it all sounded so complicated, he gave up and instead asked, 'Is that really how it worked, sir?'

'Believe it or not, it was, Dewbush.'

'And did they keep asking you if you wanted to buy something else all the time, like they do now, sir?'

'Not then, Dewbush, no. That sort of thing only happened at fast food restaurants.'

There was another pause, a much longer one this time, before Dewbush asked, 'Did you have to catch your own food when you went to a restaurant, sir?'

'Sorry, Dewbush, I'm not with you.'

'You said the restaurants had fast food, sir. Did you have to catch it?'

'Er, no, Dewbush. The food itself wasn't fast. The term was given to certain restaurants who cooked the food when you were actually there.'

'But didn't all restaurants cook the food when you were there, sir?'

'Well, yes, I suppose they did. It's just that some cooked it faster than others, and the ones that did called it "fast food".'

Dewbush thought about that for a moment before asking, 'So, did some restaurants deliberately cook their food really slowly, sir?'

Fortunately for Capstan, who was beginning to feel mentally drained by the whole conversation, he suddenly saw two people dressed in long black coats and wearing bright red crash helmets walk out from the side of the house that the YouGet truck was parked outside.

'Any idea who they are, Dewbush?'

'I'm not sure, sir. Hold on,' and he reached inside his suit jacket pocket, pulled out his touch-tech glasses and put them on.

'Well, we've found Miss Butterbum, sir. She's the one on the left. The other one is Finley Farthington, otherwise known as Starstrider. He's twenty-one years old and is a final year student at Cambridge University where he's studying Intergalactic Law. He's currently single, he's a Sagittarius, his favourite colour is blue, and when he's not studying he likes playing video games and going to the cinema. His favourite game at the moment is *Zombies Warmed Up: It's Cooking Time*, and the last film he went to see was *The Milkman: No Swap-Backs*. He's a founding member of the Intergalactic Free Rangers and has no criminal record, but he does have nine points on his driver's licence.'

Capstan stared at Dewbush.

'Do you know him, Lieutenant?' he asked, with the worrying feeling that his subordinate had just inadvertently given the game away, and that he too was somehow involved in this missing girl/stolen cow case.

'Do I know who, sir?'

'The man on the right?'

'I don't think so, sir. Why?'

'So how d'you know so much about him then?'

'Oh, I see! No, sir,' replied Dewbush, taking his glasses off and holding them up. 'These are

142

Photochromic Touch-Tech VRs, sir. They use virtual reality to overlay a full bio of the person you're looking at, and they have a UKA police upgrade which gives a further summary of any convictions. You've got a similar pair yourself, sir.'

'But isn't that an invasion of people's privacy?' asked Capstan, as he reached inside for the pair the Duty Officer had given him but which he'd yet to try on.

'Er, of course, sir, but that's how we meet other people and get sold stuff we might need, sir.'

Capstan did a bit of a double-take between his touch-tech glasses and his subordinate.

'So, you're telling me that anyone can put these on, look at me, and know all there is to know?'

'No, sir. They won't tell you all there is to know about everything, sir. Just everything there is to know about *you*. They'd need to look at other things to find out everything there is to know about them, sir.'

'But is there nothing I can do to stop it?'

'You could always change your privacy settings, sir, but not many people want to.'

'Well, I do! How can I do that?'

'You should be able to access them through your touch-tech PalmPad, sir.'

'My touch-tech what?' asked Capstan, feeling older by the minute.

'Your touch-tech PalmPad, sir. The device you were

given with the watch and the glasses.' But Capstan still looked none-the-wiser, so he added, 'The one you hold in your hand, sir.'

'Oh, you mean the phone thing,' said Capstan, putting the glasses away and pulling out his touch-tech PalmPad instead.

'If you say so, sir, but your phone is actually what you're wearing on your wrist.'

Trying to focus on one gadget at a time, and with his touch-tech PalmPad now in his hands, Capstan asked, 'So, how do I adjust my privacy settings?'

'Shall I try and do it for you, sir?'

'If you could, yes please,' and he handed it over to his Lieutenant.

'What setting do you want, sir?'

'What's the choice?'

'High, medium or low?'

'That's straight forward enough, I suppose. And does "high" stand for very private?'

'It does, sir, yes, but people will still be able to know your name, date of birth, star sign, your marital status and what your favourite colour is, sir.'

'Well, I suppose that will have to do.'

'Right you are, sir. Here you go,' and Dewbush handed the touch-tech device back to Capstan.

'Thank you, Dewbush.' As Capstan put it back into his inside suit jacket pocket he looked up and said, 'Where did they go?'

'Where did who go, sir?'

'Lucy Butterbum and her little friend.'

'I've no idea, sir. They were there a minute ago.'

'Well, we'd better find them then, hadn't we!'

'Yes, sir.' Dewbush pulled out his own touch-tech PalmPad, turned it on, swiped at the screen a few times, looked up and over to his right and said, 'They're over there, sir.'

'And what are they doing over there?' asked Capstan, who couldn't see as Dewbush's head was in the way.

'It looks like they're waiting for a bus, sir.'

'A bus?'

'I think so, sir, yes.'

'And they have busses on Titan, do they?'

'Of course, sir. How else would they get around?'

'I've no idea, Dewbush. I suppose I thought that maybe they'd spend their entire day flying about in the air?'

'Er, the buses do spend their entire day flying about in the air, sir,' and he pointed upwards. 'There's one coming down now.'

'Right then,' said Capstan, as he leaned forward to watch what did look almost exactly like a flying bus hover in over their car and land beside a round red sign that had the words BOSI DURO written in capital letters on it.

'Shall we follow them, sir?' asked Dewbush.

'If they get on it, I think we should, yes. And hopefully they'll then lead us straight to the cow, and the people they must have sold it to.'

CHAPTER TWENTY ONE

A S STARSTRIDER helped Lucy onto the bus for their day trip to Titania, and as Capstan and Dewbush followed along behind, hoping to be led to where the stolen cow had been stashed, President Müller asked his Vice President, Samuel Pollock, to meet Lord Von Splotitty at the Ronald McDoughnut Intergalactic Airport in Washington, which was the only place big enough for Splotitty's starship to land. Müller's intention was for Samuel Pollock to give Splotitty a gift box containing a copy of the video, as a little keepsake and to serve as a reminder of the night before.

Pollock had been serving as Müller's Vice President since he won the election to become what was then called the President of the United States of America, back in the year 2340. It was just one year later that Müller had taken over the World, and the year after that he'd been able to have the 22nd Amendment changed so that he could serve for more than two four-year terms. At first, he'd only been able to persuade Congress to extend it to three terms, and they'd only agreed because he'd done such a good job at taking over the World on their behalf. But after he'd been President of Earth for eleven years, when he asked for it to be extended to four terms, he'd sent his Secret Service Agents out to assassinate anyone who dared say anything other than the extension to his Presidency was the best idea they'd ever heard since someone put a slice of bread under a grill and called it toast.

For Samuel Pollock, that meant President Müller was now in his 30th term in office, and with a human's average life expectancy increasing by the day, he'd recently come to the conclusion that if he was ever going to get promoted to being President of Earth himself, he was going to have to do something about it, other than sit around waiting for Müller to keel over from natural causes. With that in mind, he'd requested a private meeting with Lord Von Splotitty, with the promise of reaching an agreement that if they would help him to usurp the incumbent President, he, as Earth's brand new President, would make sure they got the trade deal they wanted.

But all that had backfired in two ways. Firstly, President Müller had told him to agree to whatever it was that Splotitty asked for, something he'd not expected him to do in a million years, and which left him with not a whole lot to have a clandestine meeting about. Secondly, he was told about the compromising video, a copy of which was on the memory projector stick inside the elaborately decorated wooden gift box that he held in his hands as he stood beside a red carpet next to the ramp leading up to Splotitty's starship. As he waited there, between his two bodyguards, to make the formal presentation of the box, and the memory projector stick inside it, and as he watched Lord Von Splotitty waddle his way towards him like a fat pregnant duck, all he could do was hope to God that he wouldn't look inside the box when he handed it to him.

When Splotitty stopped beside him, the Vice President of Earth bowed with dutiful reverence, and knowing that he was being filmed by the intergalactic media, and therefore that his President would be watching, he held out his hands to present the gift box.

Taking it from him, Splotitty looked down at it; but, fortunately for Pollock, he didn't open it. Instead, he passed it back to one of his own bodyguards. Then he leaned in towards Pollock and whispered, 'If I could have a word with you, in private, I'd be most tremendously grateful.'

With his head still facing down at the red carpet, Pollock replied, 'Of course, Lord Von Splotitty.' He looked up, dismissed his two bodyguards, and proceeded to walk with him onto the ramp of the giant-sized spaceship, which looked pretty-much like everything else associated with Titan in that it was large and pink, and bore more than a passing resemblance to a moulded pudding best served cold, straight from the fridge.

As they approached the airtight door set within the starship's fuselage, he was desperately hoping that his President wasn't watching, and if he was, that he didn't think it was too strange a sight to see him walking side by side with the Supreme High Councillor of Titan, Commander in Chief of the Mammary Clans, straight into his blancmange-shaped starship.

Inside, Pollock was led into a generously sized circular cabin, in the centre of which was an enormous waterbed covered with purple and pink sheets. On top of that sprawled what Pollock assumed to be a female of the species, as she wore bright purple lipstick and had a little too much mascara around each of her four eyes.

Splotitty looked at her and said, 'O le jowo lo kuro. A nilo lati soro ni ikoko.'

The moulded pudding-shaped female life form began to roll and bounce herself off the bed until she could stand up, at which point she said, 'Dajudaju Mo ti le darlin. Mo ti le gba o mejeji kan gilasi ti wara nigba ti Mo wa kuro?'

Turning to Pollock, Splotitty said, 'My wife is asking if you would like a glass of milk?'

'Oh, thank you. That's very kind of you. Yes please!'

Turning back to the pink blob who was apparently his wife, Splotitty commanded, 'Oun yoo, o Ṣeun owOn!'

The girl blob blinked her understanding with her eyes and smiled at their guest before folding herself over in a brave attempt at a bow. She then waddled her way out of the cabin, closing the wide double-doors behind her as she went.

Returning his gaze to Pollock, Splotitty said, 'So, we are alone!'

Pollock gulped. He'd not thought this through, and realised that he should have declined his guest's kind offer of coming on board his starship; either that or he should have at least insisted that he was accompanied by his two bodyguards.

Splotitty looked at him and said, 'You look worried.'

'I'm not worried.'

'Good. You don't need to be worried.'

'Well, I'm not.'

'Great, but don't you think you should be?'

'Why should I be worried?'

'No reason. Anyway,' continued Splotitty, 'I merely wanted to invite you up here to ask for your advice.'

'I'm happy to help in any way I can.'

'I assume you know about what happened this morning?'

'It was a very regrettable incident, yes.'

'And you knew nothing about it?'

Horrified by the very suggestion, Pollock said, 'Of

course not! I'm on your side, remember?'

'Well, that's good to hear. So, now I find myself in an awkward position, and I was wondering if you could be so kind as to suggest some way that I could get myself out of it.'

'Oh, er, well. I'm not sure, really.'

'Let me put it another way. If you don't help me, I'll eat you.'

Pollock gulped once again.

'Um, well, I suppose you could try and turn the tables on him.'

'And what use is a table in such a situation?'

'No use, really. It was just a figure of speech. What I meant was that you could doeth unto him what he hath doneth unto you.'

'What?'

'An eye for an eye, and a tooth for a tooth.'

'I've got no idea what you're going on about, but I am, however, becoming increasingly hungry.'

Realising he'd better stop using proverbial metaphors and get to the point, Pollock said, 'If you invite him to your planet, get him drunk, leave him in a room full of prostitutes, and film everything that happens, you'd be equal!'

Another wide smile spread out over Splotitty's face.

'You see, Pollock. I always knew you'd be able to come up with something,' and with that he waddled his way over to a nearby desk, pressed a large purple button on it with his short thick tentacle, and said, 'Ṣe o gba Aare ti Earth, Dick Müller, lori foonu fun mi jọwọ?'

Immediately a voice came back over the intercom saying, '*Otun kuro,* Olanla Re,' and a moment or two later, none other than Dick Müller's voice came on the line.

'Hello Timmy! Have you decided to hand over Titan to me yet?'

'President Müller, how good of you to take my call.'

'No problem at all, Timmy. So, is it Titan, or an intergalactic broadcast of whatever it was that you were getting up to last night?'

'And that is what I wanted to discuss with you, President Müller.'

'Oh, really? I wasn't aware that the subject was up for discussion.'

Doing his best to ignore him, Splotitty went on, 'I have with me, on board my starship, your Vice President, Samuel Pollock.'

'Well done, but I'm not sure of the relevance.'

'Pollock has suggested that it would help if you could come over to Titan to discuss the terms of our…surrender.'

There was a pause whilst Müller thought about that for a moment, before saying, 'No can do, Timmy, I'm quite happy here, thank you very much. And besides, I really don't think there's anything to talk about. Either you hand over Titan to me, or I hand over the video to the Intergalactic News Federation.'

'But what if I were to tell you that we'd kidnapped your Vice President, and that the talks were to discuss the terms of his release.'

There was another pause from the end of the phone, during which Splotitty stared over at Pollock, who didn't look particularly comfortable with the situation he seemed to have found himself in.

'That's an interesting proposal, really it is,' said President Müller. 'However, I've got Fred Fortune as our Speaker of the House, and he'd probably make a better Vice President than Pollock. So I suggest you keep him.'

'I don't think you'll think the same thing when we take him to our planet and start pulling his arms and legs off, live on TV.'

'I suppose that depends which network you'd use to broadcast it on.'

'What's that got to do with it?' asked Splotitty.

'It's just that I've only got Galaxy Premium Plus,' replied President Müller, 'and I'd hate to miss it.'

'So you're saying that you're happy for us to take your Vice President with us?'

'Help yourself, Timmy. Tell you what, I'm even happy to wait for you to get him back on Titan and start pulling his arms and legs off before I hand over the tape to the Intergalactic News Federation. How does that sound?'

'FINE!' shouted Splotitty, and slapped his tentacle down hard on the same purple button, ending the call. He then turned to Pollock, and through gritted teeth, of which he had rather a lot, said, 'So, it looks like you're coming with us, and perhaps, on our way, you can explain to me why he keeps calling me Timmy all the time. It's not my name, and it's becoming rather annoying.'

CHAPTER TWENTY TWO

MEANWHILE, back on Titan, Lucy and Starstrider stepped onto the bus, as Capstan suspected they would, and Dewbush drove off after them, set with the task of following the bus in such a way that neither Lucy nor Starstrider would suspect that they were being followed.

As it crawled its way along a road lined on either side with an apparently endless number of semi-detached dome-shaped houses, stopping to land at each bus stop along the way to pick up a variety of pink blancmange-shaped life forms, Dewbush asked, 'Did you use to follow suspects around like this, sir, back in the 21st Century?'

'Of course, Lieutenant. It was all part of the job.'

'And was my great-great-great-great-grandfather with you, sir, when you did?'

As Capstan stared out of the window at some of the peculiar creatures he was seeing as they waddled about their business in a variety of ill-fitting brightly-coloured clothes, he remembered one particular instance back on Earth in a place called Bath, when he'd first been assigned to work with Dewbush's long-deceased relative. That was before they'd both been re-located down to Portsmouth. It had been their first case, during which Capstan had told Dewbush to follow a suspect called Becky Phillips, an attractive young lady who'd been involved in a local bank robbery. To do so he'd disguised Dewbush as a woman, after he'd bought him a dress, some stilettoes, and a wig from a charity shop. Capstan remembered what he'd been told had happened in a department store on the high street, where Dewbush had apparently been caught spying on the suspect as she was trying on some lingerie in the ladies' changing room. He shuddered, and answered, 'Not always, Dewbush, No. Sometimes we'd follow people around independently, in order to make the best use of our time and resources.'

'Did you ever follow a bus, sir?'

'With your great-great-great-great-grandfather?'

'Yes, sir. Like we're doing now, sir.'

Thinking back again, Capstan said, 'I can't remember having ever followed a bus before, Dewbush, but we may have done.'

There was a lull in the conversation as they continued to follow the bus and as the street grew ever busier, with a growing number of floating cars all jostling for position down both sides of the road while the occasional blancmange-shaped life-form risked life and tentacle trying to cross it.

'I don't suppose you could tell me about some of the cases you worked on together, at some point, could you, sir?' asked Dewbush, feeling a little shy about asking as it felt more like a personal matter than one relating specifically to space police business.

'At some point, Dewbush, I will, but in the meantime, may I suggest you try to keep a little bit more distance between ourselves and the bus?'

Just as he'd said that, it braked hard in front of them, forcing Dewbush to do an emergency stop in a bid to avoid driving straight into the back of it.

'Sorry about that, sir.'

'If you'd kept your distance, Dewbush, it wouldn't have happened.'

'I'm trying to, sir. But it's not easy when it keeps stopping all the time.'

'It's a bus, Dewbush. That's what they do.'

'Yes, sir.'

'Tell you what. Why don't you try to keep one of the other cars between us and the bus?'

'But what would I do when it stops again, sir? Surely I'd have to pull up behind it whilst the other car overtook, and then I'd be back where I was, sir.'

Dewbush had a point, and Capstan tried to think back to his police training, to see if he could remember being taught how to follow a suspect by car after they'd hopped onto a bus. But he couldn't recall the subject having ever come up, which meant that either it hadn't been included in the syllabus, or he'd been off sick that day. And as he was fairly sure he'd never followed one himself before, he said, 'Just do the best you can, Dewbush. Hopefully they'll be getting off soon.'

'Right you are, sir.'

And it wasn't long before the two suspects did exactly that; and as Dewbush pulled up behind the bus again, this time in an actual parking space, Capstan went to open the door.

Seeing what he was about to do out of the corner of his eye, and just in time to stop him from doing it, Dewbush grabbed his arm and called out, '*NO, SIR!*'

'*What*, Dewbush?' asked Capstan. He didn't like being told what to do at the best of times, and certainly didn't liked being grabbed at the same time.

'Sorry, sir, but there's no oxygen out there. You need to put an air-helmet on before you get out.'

'Well, why didn't you tell me?'

'I just thought it was obvious, I suppose, sir. That's why the suspects are wearing those red helmets.'

Reaching behind him, Dewbush lifted up the back seat, underneath which was a compartment containing a number of items, including two large Nerf-type guns, a pair of handcuffs, a length of rope, a knife, a few gas canisters, six spherical metallic objects that looked like hand-grenades, four bottles of water, two heavy black coats, and two blue helmets.

Grabbing one of the helmets, he passed it to Capstan. 'Here you go, sir. It has well-compressed air built in which should last around eight hours.'

Taking it from him, Capstan stared at it and asked, 'And what if it runs out?'

'Then you'll have to get it filled up, sir. But don't worry. There's always somewhere you can get well-compressed air from.'

Then he leant back again and grabbed one of the coats.

'You'll need to wear this as well, sir.'

'A coat?' asked Capstan.

'It's a gravity-coat, sir. It will allow you to walk on Titan without floating around. And it will help to keep you warm as well, sir.'

'Right. So I should put these on now, should I?'

'I would if I were you, sir, else you'd just float off into space the moment you stepped out of the car to die a few minutes later from asphyxiation. You'd also probably get a little cold as well, sir.'

'Don't worry, Dewbush. You had me at "asphyxiation".'

Dewbush gave him a peculiar look, and before he decided that his superior had said something that could be considered by some to be vaguely amusing, and so give him justification for placing him under arrest, Capstan changed the subject. 'So I put my head inside here, do I?'

'That's right, Sir.'

Capstan busied himself putting his air-helmet on,

then took his seat belt off and began wriggling his way into the thick heavy black coat, which wasn't easy, being that he was sitting in the passenger side seat of an average sized space car. But it was at least easier for him than it was for Dewbush, who'd also begun to put his on but had the steering wheel to contend with.

When they were both air-helmeted and gravity-coated, Capstan remembered why they'd been getting all kitted up in the first place; they were supposed to be following Lucy and her friend. But that was a good five minutes ago.

'Did you see which way they went?' he asked Dewbush, concerned for the second time that day that they'd lost them.

'Don't worry, sir. She's still got the tracking device on her.'

'Oh yes, of course. I keep forgetting about that.'

Looking at the door handle with due caution, he asked, 'So, it's safe for me to get out now, is it?'

Dewbush quickly checked Capstan over, making sure his coat was done up properly, the air-helmet's chin strap was secure, and that the air supply had automatically started as it was supposed to. When he was happy that everything was as it should be, he said, 'It's quite safe now, sir.'

Carefully, Capstan opened his car door, stuck his head out into the chilly atmosphere beyond and tentatively breathed in. Apart from the fact that it was cold and there wasn't much light, it seemed fine, so he stepped out and closed the door behind him.

After Dewbush had locked the car with a button on his watch, and the car had doubled-bleeped to indicate that it was indeed locked, he walked around to join Capstan on the pavement, pulling out his touch-tech PalmPad as he did. There he stopped, stared down at it and called out, 'She's this way, sir,' and began wandering along the bustling high street, all the time looking at his hand-held device like a schoolboy walking through town staring at a compass in an effort to get his Duke of Edinburgh Award for Orienteering, with Capstan following closely behind.

It wasn't long before Dewbush stopped dead in his tracks and Capstan walked straight into the back of him.

'Sorry, sir, but we must have gone past them.'

Capstan stepped out of his way, and Dewbush began walking backwards, still looking down at his touch-tech PalmPad. He soon stopped again and glanced over to his left. 'They must have gone inside this restaurant, sir.'

'What should we do?' asked Capstan.

He wasn't used to asking his subordinate, either this one or the one back in the 21st Century, what they should do, but he'd never found himself standing outside a restaurant on a moon orbiting Saturn wearing an air-helmet and a gravity-coat before, and he simply didn't know.

'I suggest we go in, sir. We can keep an eye on them from there, and we'd also be able to get something to eat.'

'Good idea, Dewbush,' said Capstan, who was hungry, but more importantly, he really needed to go to the toilet. But as he'd no intention of going in first, he motioned with his hand to Dewbush, and said, 'After you!'

'Thank you, sir.' Dewbush put his touch-tech PalmPad away, pushed open the glass door and led Capstan into the building.

Inside was a large wide room that had a series of high round purple tables in the middle, none of which had any chairs, and dotted around the sides of the room were eight purple cubicle areas, all of which had seating, but four had an additional glass dome over the top.

Capstan noticed that there was a counter to his immediate left, behind which stood a pink blancmange-shaped creature that was about five feet tall, seven feet wide, had four eyes and a wide pink mouth, and was wearing a generously portioned pair of beige coloured trousers that were held up by two bright red suspenders. As the creature didn't have shoulders, not that Capstan could see, the braces just went all the way over the top of its moulded pudding-shaped head, very close to where its eyes and mouth were. The braces themselves were each lined with numerous brightly coloured badges, all with different writing on, but none of which Capstan could decipher.

Seeing that the two new patrons were human, the creature looked at them and asked, 'Table for two?'

'Yes, please?' replied Dewbush.

'Sitting down or standing up?'

'Sitting down, please.'

'Oxygenated or non-oxygenated?'

'Oh, er…' and he looked behind him at Capstan. 'Would you like an oxygenated table or a non-oxygenated table, sir?'

'Would an oxygenated table allow us to eat without having to wear these crash helmet things?' asked Capstan, as he stared around the inside of his.

'They would, sir, yes.'

'Then I think I'd prefer oxygenated.'

Turning back to the pink blob wearing the trousers with the braces, Dewbush said, 'Oxygenated, please.'

The creature smiled at Dewbush and Capstan. 'Would you follow to me, please?' and waddled off to one of the seated cubical area, one of the ones that had a glass dome over the top of it.

As Capstan and Dewbush ducked under the dome, the pink blob waiter thing went over to the wall, and with its short thick tentacle, pulled a lever down. Then it handed Capstan and Dewbush a couple of menus, saying, 'There is oxygen for you now, and I come back soon to take your order.'

With that, the blob creature waddled back to the desk it had been standing behind when they'd first come in.

After Capstan and Dewbush had taken off their air-helmets and placed them down on the seating beside them, Dewbush looked around and said, 'This is nice, isn't it, sir?'

Capstan wasn't sure what was so nice about it, other than that it was a restaurant in which they could breathe without having to wear an air-helmet. But he didn't want to seem disagreeable and so answered, 'Yes, Dewbush, very nice!' with only the slightest hint of sarcasm. 'So—have you seen them?'

'Seen who, sir?' asked Dewbush, who'd already picked up the menu and had started reading it.

'Miss Butterbum and her boyfriend?'

'I don't think he's her boyfriend, sir.'

'Either way, can you see them anywhere?'

Dewbush pulled out his touch-tech PalmPad again, swiped the screen a few times, craned his head to look over Capstan's shoulder, and said, 'Yes, sir. They're over there. Second cubicle from the right,' and went back to reading his menu.

With his right elbow on the table, Capstan rested his head in his hand as if studying the menu, before he slowly swivelled it around so that he could look at Lucy and the man she was with, without it being obvious that he was staring at them.

'They're there all right,' he confirmed, in a low, conspiratorial tone.

Without looking up from his menu, Dewbush said, 'Yes, I know, sir. Lucy's location is clearly marked on the tracker app, and not only that, sir, but we can see them.'

Capstan had to admit that he was struggling to get used to the idea that the girl had a tracking device on her which, now that he thought about it, made the idea of following her around rather pointless.

'What are you having, sir?' asked Dewbush, a moment or two later.

'Oh, er…' said Capstan, and picked up his menu to begin trying to read it. He turned it upside down and had another go, but as he still couldn't work out a single thing it said, he placed it back on the table, looked over at Dewbush and said, 'I'm not sure, Dewbush. What are you having?'

'I think I'm going to go for the Awon ewa lori Tositi.'

'And what's that, when it's at home?'

'I don't know what it is when it's at home, sir, but here it's their Earth Special of the Day. Beans on Toast, sir.'

'And that's nice, is it?' asked Capstan. He'd had beans on toast often enough when he was a boy, but he'd never liked it much, even then.

'It should be, sir!' exclaimed Dewbush.

Capstan picked up the menu again and looked at it. He didn't fancy beans on toast, but as he'd no idea what else to choose, he said, 'I suppose I'd better have the same, then.'

As Dewbush continued to study the menu, Capstan began to squirm in his seat. His need to go to the toilet was reaching breaking point.

'I don't suppose you know where the toilets are, by any chance?' he asked.

Looking up again, Dewbush stared around the restaurant until he said, 'I think they're over there, sir,' and pointed at a door in the corner.

'Oh good!' replied Capstan.

Dewbush didn't add what Capstan had hoped he would, that he also wanted to go, and simply returned to reading his menu, so Capstan was forced to clear his throat and ask, 'I don't suppose you could, er, if you'd mind...come with me, Dewbush? It's just that I've never been to the toilet anywhere else but on Earth, or back at the police space station.'

'Of course, sir. How selfish of me. Come on. We can go together!'

CHAPTER TWENTY THREE

AFTER DEWBUSH had helped Capstan go to the toilet, which wasn't as difficult as he'd thought it would be, apart from having to put their air-helmets back on, they returned to their cubicle, removed the helmets again, and enjoyed an almost pleasant main course consisting of hot baked beans that had been poured over the top of two pieces of toast. For pudding they decided to steer clear of the blancmange on offer, as the idea of eating cold moulded pudding in a restaurant on Titan seemed a little insensitive, almost barbaric. Instead they opted for two milkshakes, a strawberry one for Dewbush and a chocolate one for Capstan. They enjoyed some coffee as they waited for Lucy and her friend Starstrider to leave, then they paid their bill, put their air-helmets back on and set off after them.

They spent a pleasant day following them around, which Capstan found a lot less stressful than following suspects normally was, thanks to the tracker embedded in Lucy's thigh. So, without having to keep an eye on them all the time, they were free to take in some of the sights.

The first one they visited was Monsieur Tussauds, which was an idea that had clearly been borrowed from London's still famous Madame Tussauds, but instead of using wax models they'd used rubber ones, and instead of featuring famous people from Earth it housed various heroic members of Titan's Mammary Clans.

After Monsieur Tussauds, they went to look at Big Bill which, again, seemed very similar to one of London's tourist attractions, Big Ben. However, it was pink instead of brick coloured, it wasn't rectangular but more of a cylindrical shape, and it didn't have a clock on the top of it but just a really large purple dome, so the whole structure had a rather embarrassing phallic appearance, to Capstan's eye at least.

The last sight they went to see was called The Statue of Mammary, which Capstan thought may have been inspired by New York's famous Statue of Liberty, but he couldn't be sure. It just looked like a giant-sized moulded pudding made of iron with a torch sticking out of it, like a chocolate flake stuck into a Mr Whippy ice cream.

After spending half an hour at The Statue of Mammary, during which time Dewbush showed Capstan how to take a picture of it using his touch-tech PalmPad, they followed Lucy and Starstrider back to a bus stop and watched them head off. By then Capstan had become used to the idea of not having to keep them in sight at all times, and they ambled their way back to find their police car at a leisurely pace.

There they picked up Lucy's signal again and followed it, only to find themselves right back where they'd started, outside the domed-shaped semi-detached house which still had the YouGet delivery truck parked outside. But by then that wasn't the only thing outside the house. A sign had been stuck in the front garden which had a rather crude drawing of a cow with a speech bubble coming out of its mouth that said, "Moo". Above that was written "Titan Àkọkọ Lailai Free Range Maalu Zoo" and underneath the English translation; "Titan's First Ever Free Range Cow Zoo". Sitting behind a desk next to the sign was another figure wearing a black gravity-coat and a red air-helmet, and in front of the desk began an enormous queue of Mammary Clans that stretched right the way around the block, all of whom seemed rather keen to get their very first glimpse of an actual real-life Earth cow.

As Dewbush focused on landing their unmarked police space car behind the YouGet delivery truck, Capstan stared out at the scene, trying to work out what was going on, and why there were so many lifeforms there; but it was only when he saw the sign that he was able to figure it out, and what that meant for their case.

'The cow must be here, Dewbush!' he exclaimed,

with some excitement.

'What makes you say that, sir?' asked Dewbush, as he landed the car and joined Capstan in staring out the window.

'That sign. Can you see it? They've started a Cow Zoo! That must be why they stole the cow!'

'Do you think so, sir?'

'Of course I think so, Dewbush! C'mon, we've faffed about here for quite long enough. Let's get out, find the cow, and then we can arrest the lot of them.'

'Great idea, sir!' said Dewbush, and after they'd both put their air-helmets back on, they stepped out of the car and marched over towards the queue of Mammary Clans at the front of the house.

Barging their way to the front, they saw Lucy and Starstrider chatting with the person sitting behind the desk. With the help of his Photochromic Touch-Tech VR glasses, it only took Dewbush a moment to identify that person as a Mr Oberon O'Brian who was currently single, whose favourite colour was red, was a final year student at Cambridge University like Starstrider, and, of most interest to Capstan and Dewbush, was also an Intergalactic Free Ranger with responsibility for both accounts and marketing.

As they approached the table, Capstan pulled out his UKA Space Police ID, held it up and called out, 'Miss Butterbum, it's Detective Inspector Capstan and Sergeant Dewbush.'

'Oh! Hello, you two! What are you doing here?'

'Your father reported you as missing, Miss Butterbum,' continued Capstan, 'possibly kidnapped, and we've been tasked with the job of finding you and bringing you home.'

'That's certainly very kind of you. But as you can see, I'm here, safe and sound, I haven't been kidnapped, and you can tell my father that I'll go back to Earth when I feel like it.'

'We also need to talk to you about the stolen cow, Miss Butterbum.'

'Oh yes, what about it?' she asked, glancing over at Starstrider standing beside her.

'Do you know where it is?'

'Er. I'm not sure. Why?'

'We have reason to believe, Miss Butterbum, that you're directly involved in its theft.'

'She had nothing to do with it!' protested Starstrider, taking a protective step forward. 'We just happened to take Lucy with us when we were liberating the second cow.'

'The second cow?' asked Capstan. 'So you've stolen two of them?'

'No!' said Starstrider. 'We've *liberated* two of them, so saving them from the cruel oppressive practices of Earth's modern day intensive farming methods.'

'Right, but that's still stealing though, isn't it!' stated Capstan.

'No, it isn't, *actually!*'

'I think it is,' said Capstan, but not sounding quite so sure that time. If he'd been back on Earth in the 21st Century he'd have been more certain, but on Titan, in the 25th Century, he really wasn't, and glanced over at Dewbush for help.

'I'm sure you're right, sir,' confirmed Dewbush, as he pulled out his touch-tech PalmPad in order to look up exactly what the law said about it.

However, Starstrider was of a different opinion.

'You're both wrong!' he declared, 'and I should know because I'm a final year Intergalactic Law student at Cambridge University!'

He gave both policemen a defiant look of smug contempt, but as neither seemed as impressed as he thought they should have been, launched into an elaboration of his legal reasoning.

'Stealing is only stealing when you sell whatever it is that you've taken. We haven't stolen the cows because we've released them here, on Titan, where they're allowed to roam free, not locked in a cage miles beneath the ground being endlessly milked for no other reason than commercial gain. So, as we haven't sold them to anyone, it's not theft!'

By then Dewbush had found the relevant section of the law, and began to read it out.

'Section one of the Intergalactic Theft Act 2378 states that a lifeform is guilty of theft if he, she, or it, dishonestly appropriates property belonging to another with intention to permanently deprive the other lifeform of it. It doesn't say anything about whether or not that lifeform has to go on to sell whatever it was that they'd taken.'

'That must be in a later section,' said Starstrider, still not convinced.

'So, anyway,' interrupted Capstan, who didn't see his role as an interpreter of the law, just the guy whose job it was to arrest people who'd broken it. 'Where are the cows now?' Once he found them, as far as he was concerned that would be proof enough.

'They're in the back garden,' admitted Starstrider.

'Right!' said Capstan. 'C'mon Dewbush, let's take a look round the back,' and he marched off towards the side of the house where he'd seen Lucy and Starstrider emerge when they'd first spotted them earlier that day.

CHAPTER TWENTY FOUR

A S CAPSTAN ENTERED the back garden with Dewbush following behind, over the tops of a group of about ten Mammary Clans taking photographs he could see that the two cows were there all right, both wearing breathing apparatus and gravity-blankets. They seemed content enough, though clearly trying to solve the problem of the grass and why neither seemed able to eat it.

Standing in front of the cows was another person wearing a black gravity-coat and a red air-helmet who Dewbush was able to identify, with the aid of his glasses, as a Mr Calisto Clumpton. According to public records Calisto was single, his favourite colour was green, he was another final year student at Cambridge University and furthermore, was an Intergalactic Free Ranger, responsible for driving and navigation.

Pushing his way through the crowd, Capstan marched straight up to the man and with an accusatory tone asked, 'Are these your cows?'

'Er,' he replied, as though not exactly sure.

'Right!' said Capstan, 'We're taking them as material evidence.' He then stepped over to the nearest one and took hold of the strap that held its breathing mask on, calling out behind him, 'Grab the other one,

Dewbush!'

As Capstan began leading it towards the side gate, Dewbush said, 'Right you are, sir,' and took hold of the second cow in exactly the same way as his boss had done and started to heave at it in a bid to persuade it to move. But this cow didn't seem to be as compliant as the other one, and just remained where it was, still trying to feed itself on the lush green grass that was spread out before it like a medieval vegetarian banquet that had been cursed by a passing wizard, making it impossible for it to be eaten.

'And what do you think you're doing?' asked Lucy, who'd followed Capstan and Dewbush around to the back of the house along with Starstrider and Oberon O'Brian, as well as a good portion of the front of the Mammary Clan queue who, with nobody at the ticket desk, had surged forward to find out what was going on and to hopefully get a free glimpse of a real life Earth cow.

'We're taking these as material evidence in the case of the stolen cows,' announced Capstan, 'which reminds me,' and he looked over at Dewbush, who'd now begun pulling as hard as he could at the cow's oxygen mask in a bid to persuade his one to move. 'Dewbush, if you could be so kind as to place this lot under arrest, I'd be very grateful.'

'Give me just one minute, sir,' Dewbush replied through gritted teeth, as he dug his heels into the artificial grass and heaved at the cow's mask with all his might. But instead of the cow budging, the strap holding its mask on broke, and Dewbush fell over backwards, with the cow's breathing apparatus entangled around his hands.

As the growing crowd gave out a collective gasp, the sound of which encouraged even more of the queue to surge around to the back of the house, Capstan asked, 'What on earth are you doing, Dewbush?'

'Sorry, sir. The strap must have broken.'

But the cow didn't seem to mind at all. Finding the curse of the medieval vegetarian banquet to have lifted, it was now free to eat as much of the florescent green grass as it possibly could, and began grazing away. But it didn't take long for it to realise two things; firstly that the grass tasted more like a green plastic water bottle that had been run over by a lawnmower than actual grass, and secondly that for some strange reason it was unable to breathe. And as it began lifting its head up and down like an old American oil pump in an effort to do so, Starstrider yelled, 'IT NEEDS AIR, YOU IDIOT! PUT ITS MASK BACK ON!!!'

Dewbush stood up, and began attempting to untangle the mask from around his hands as Lucy, Starstrider and the other two members of the Intergalactic Free Rangers sprinted over to help; but five people trying to wrestle a cow's oxygen mask off

177

just one person was even less effective than one person trying to do it on his own. But by then it was too late anyway, as the cow breathed its last breath and keeled over onto its side like a rectangular shaped tree that had just been cut down in order to make a flat-packed wardrobe.

A stunned silence fell over the back garden of the semi-detached house on the outskirts of Titania, as everyone stared down at what just moments before had been Titan's most sacred species of animal, but was now simply 725 kg of ready meals and leather furniture just waiting to be mass produced.

It didn't take long for shock to turn to anger, as the ever-growing number of Mammary Clans who had been piling into the back garden began pointing with their various shaped tentacles at first the cow, and then the humans who for some unknown reason had taken it upon themselves to murder it. And as a collective wobbling mass, they started to call out, 'APANIA! MIMO MAALU APANIA! PA AWON MIMO MAALU APANIA!' as they encircled the six humans like red Indians surrounding an overturned stage coach that had just run over the burial site of one of their ancient dead relatives.

'I don't suppose anyone knows what they're saying, by any chance?' asked Capstan.

Fortunately Calisto was reading Intergalactic Languages at Cambridge, and his specialist subject just happened to be Titanese.

'I think they're saying, "Murderers. Sacred cow murderers. Kill the sacred cow murderers",' he answered, 'but I might be wrong. The word "pa" can be translated as either "to sacrifice" or "to kill", depending on the implied meaning.'

'And is there any chance that their definition of the word sacrifice could be any different from our definition of the word sacrifice?' asked Capstan.

'Unfortunately not. A traditional Mammary Clan human sacrifice normally involves pulling the subject's arms and legs off before the internal organs are scooped out and used to make an omelette.'

'That doesn't sound so bad,' commented Dewbush, as he pulled out his gun and started trying to decide which one he'd shoot first.

'*Really?*' asked Capstan, understanding by then that there was no way he could have been joking.

'Well, I mean, it *does* sound bad, of course, sir. But it doesn't sound as bad as say being burnt alive, for example, which must be *really* bad.'

'I knew a man who was burnt alive,' interjected Starstrider, as the six of them formed a defensive circle. 'It was our school's caretaker. He was trying to light the bonfire on Guy Fawkes Night, but it wouldn't take. I suspect the wood was too damp. So he got a ladder, climbed to the top, and poured a can of liquid hydrogen over the top of it.'

'Did that work?' asked Dewbush.

'It did the trick all right. The thing went up like a rocket, but unfortunately with him still perched at the top.'

'And did he get a chance to say what it felt like?' asked Dewbush again.

'Not in so many words, no, but he did say, Aaaarrrgggghhhhh for quite a long time, so it probably was rather painful. But I can't say how it would compare to having your arms and legs pulled off.'

By this time Capstan wasn't feeling well, and was just about to ask everyone if they wouldn't mind changing the subject when he heard the chimes of what sounded almost exactly like an ice cream van approaching from somewhere above their heads.

Looking up, Calisto announced, 'It's the Rozzers!"

'The who?' asked Capstan.

'The Titan Police!'

'What, in a flying ice cream van?'

'No, you're right,' continued Calisto. 'It's not the police. It's their specialist crime prevention unit.'

'Well, it looks like they're just in the nick of time!' said Capstan, who'd taken the rather extreme measure of pulling his own gun out and aiming it at some of the surrounding lifeforms, but he still had no idea how to shoot it.

But Starstrider didn't think they were in the nick of time at all, and with a menacing scowl said to Capstan,

'But not in time to prevent you from murdering a cow, though!'

'I'm sure my Lieutenant had no intention of deliberately killing the cow, did you Dewbush?'

'Not at all, sir!'

'That's as maybe,' continued Starstrider, 'but that only brings the charge of murder down to manslaughter.'

With his free hand, Dewbush pulled out his touch-tech PalmPad again. 'I think technically it would be classified as cow-slaughter, being that no men were killed in the process, and it says here that that's not a crime, as long as the animal is used to produce ready meals and leather furniture within a 24 hour period of its demise.'

As he said that, the Mammary Clan Crime Prevention Unit descended down onto the back garden, forcing one half of the angry mob to move backwards to make room for them. And it was then that three large moulded pudding-shaped creatures wearing dark-purple uniforms stepped down out of what really did look like an ice cream van, with the one in the middle saying, 'Hello hello hello, ohun ti n lo lori nibi ki o si?' as it looked first at the dead cow, then at the angry mob, and then at the six human lifeforms, all still wearing their gravity-coats and air-helmets.

Looking around at Calisto, Capstan asked, 'I don't suppose you could translate that for us, could you?'

'He said, "Hello hello hello, what's going on here then?"'

'And is he deliberately trying to be funny?'

'In what way?' asked Calisto.

'Never mind. Just tell him that we're from Earth's UKA Space Police and that we're here to impound these two cows, and arrest these four people on suspicion of theft.'

Calisto thought for a minute, took a deep breath, and said, 'Awon wonyi ni gbigbe eda eniyan ni o wa lati Earth ká UKA Space olopa ati the've wá si to impound wonyi meji malu ati mu mi ati awon ore mi fun ole. Ṣugbon a se ko, irin awon malu, nitori a ti ko tà won, ati awon wonyi meji UKA Space Policemen ti o kan bruttally pa okan ninu awon malu!'

The three Mammary Clan police lifeforms gave Capstan and Dewbush what seemed to be a menacing sort of a look.

'They don't look very happy,' said Dewbush.

'No, they don't,' agreed Capstan. 'What exactly did you say to them?'

'Just what you said.'

'Yes, but it sounded quite a bit longer than what I'd said.'

'OK, yes, I did add a bit about you and your colleague brutally murdering the cow, but apart from that, the rest was a word for word translation.'

Capstan turned his head and gave Calisto his own version of a menacing look.

'Otun, o Pupo, ti o ba nbo pelu wa!' called out the larger Mammary Clan police lifeform, and the three members of Titan's Crime Prevention Unit began herding the six humans towards the back of their police ice cream van.

'What did he say that time?' asked Capstan, although he could probably guess.

With a disgruntled look, Calisto mumbled, 'He said, "Right, you lot, you're coming with us."'

'Shall we shoot them, sir?' asked Dewbush.

'I really don't think that would be a good idea, Lieutenant,' said Capstan, and held out his gun for the largest member of Titan's Crime Prevention Unit to take.

As Dewbush did the same, he said, 'Don't worry, sir. Section 674 of Intergalactic Law says that members of one species' police force aren't allowed to arrest the members of another without due cause, sir.'

'I think that may be where the cow comes in, Dewbush,' said Capstan, looking down at its carcass as they walked past it.

'But it's not a crime to kill a cow, sir!'

'It is on Titan!' said Calisto.

'But only if you do it on purpose,' added Dewbush.

As they were all bundled into the back of the van, Capstan asked, 'Are people who've been arrested still allowed to make a phone call, Dewbush?'

'They should be, sir, yes.'

'Then I suggest we give the Chief Inspector a call just as soon as we get to wherever it is that they're taking us.'

'Great idea, sir! I'm sure he'll be able to pull some knobs and blow some whistles to get us off the hook, sir.'

CHAPTER TWENTY FIVE

IT WASN'T LONG after Inspector Capstan, Lieutenant Dewbush, Lucy Butterbum and the three members of the Intergalactic Free Rangers had been arrested for suspected sacred cow murder by Titan's Crime Prevention Unit that Lord Von Splotitty arrived back at his palace on Titan, the Nla Aafin, which was basically a pink replica of India's Taj Mahal.

As he wobbled and bobbed down his starship's ramp towards a welcoming party made up of his homeland security team, his top level government ministers, and a fair proportion of the intergalactic press, there was only one thing on his mind: the man who was turning out to be his nemesis, The President of Earth, Dick Müller IV.

Walking beside him, as best he could, was Earth's Vice President, Mr Samuel Pollock, who'd spent the vast proportion of the trip confined to the guest quarters with only a mini bar for company, the contents of which consisted solely of tiny bottles of malt whisky and similar sized bottles of milk. Unable to stop worrying about his impending death, he'd drunk each and every one of the bottles of whisky within the first half hour of being locked in the room. Having done so, much to his annoyance he still kept visualising the scene of him having his arms and legs pulled off live on intergalactic TV, and in desperation, he'd taken to the bottles of milk as well. But the combination of the two hadn't agreed with him and he'd spent the final half hour of the trip being sick down what the Titans called an Igbonse, which on Earth was simply a toilet without either a bowl or a seat, one that a human would have to squat over to use, unless you were a man doing a wee of course, or virtually any average sized lifeform that for any reason had to throw-up the contents of its stomach, singular or plural, depending on how many stomachs the lifeform may have.

As he staggered his way down the ramp beside Lord Von Splotitty who'd effectively kidnapped him, the fact that he now had to wear a cumbersome air-helmet and an uncomfortable gravity-coat really wasn't helping his general feeling of well-being, and apart from being concerned about having his arms and legs pulled off, at that stage he was more worried about what would happen if he was sick inside his helmet.

First to greet Lord Von Splotitty at the base of the ramp was the Head of Titan's Military, Field Marshal Ofeefee, who was wearing a khaki green toga with a green beret perched on top of his head. As he wobbled up to greet his own Commander-in-Chief, he attempted a bow and said, 'Kaabo ile, Olanla Re. O le iya re wara nigbagbogbo ṣàn ninu re gbogbo itosona,' which was the traditional greeting of the Mammary Clans: 'May your mother's milk always flow in your general direction.'

'Ati tire,' replied Splotitty.

Field Marshal Ofeefee straightened himself up again, saying, 'Olanla Re, nigbati nwon ti a ti ya sinu ihamo die ninu awon eda eniyan ti o ti wa ni wi pe ohun Earth Maalu on Titan.'

'Oh dear, oh dear, oh dear,' said Splotitty, and tutting to himself turned to look at Pollock, now standing beside him.

'Did you hear that, Mr Vice President?'

'I did, Lord Von Splotitty, but unfortunately I couldn't understand it as I don't speak Titanese.'

'Good point,' and turning to his Field Marshal, said, 'As we've discussed, Ofeefee, can we please keep to English in the presence of the human species?'

'Of course, Olanla Re. I was just saying that whilst you were away, some humans killed an Earth cow here on Titan, and we're currently holding them in custardy.'

'That is very bad news indeed,' said Pollock, though it actually sounded like the best news he'd heard all day; and with just a glimmer of hope that his moulded pudding-shaped kidnapper may decide to pull the arms and legs off the cow murderers before starting on him, he asked, 'And may I enquire how many of them were arrested?'

'We arrested six humans, two of whom are members of Earth's UKA Space Police!'

'That is great—I-I mean really bad news,' said Pollock, unable to stop a thin but discernible smile from creeping over his face.

'Well, well, well, well, well, well, well!' said Splotitty. 'Now that is, how do you say, a turnip for the books.'

'Absolutely!' agreed Pollock, 'although I think the correct phrase is a turn-*up* for the books.'

'Yes, a turn-up for the books does sound better. Thank you, Mr Vice President, for pointing that out to me.'

'It was my pleasure, Lord Von Splotitty.'

'Hopefully, this news will mean that we'll be able to have a little more time together for you to teach me more of the nuisances of the English language.'

'I hope so too,' said Pollock, with genuine sincerity, 'although, again, I think you meant *nuances* as opposed to *nuisances*,' he added, hoping that if he could continue to be of service as Lord Von Splotitty's personal English teacher, he may yet survive his current predicament, and more than that, with a bit of luck he might even get paid as well, possibly allowing him to draw two salaries at the same time.

'I see,' said Splotitty. 'And may I enquire what the word nuisances means?'

'It describes things that are annoying, Lord Von Splotitty.'

'Ah! Like your Commander-in-Chief?'

'Oh, er, well, I suppose some people could say that he can be a little irksome, at times,' he said, with as much diplomacy as possible as he was very much aware that not only were they not in a private secure room, but that they were currently surrounded by about half of the intergalactic press, all holding out touch-tech PalmPads which were well-known for their ability to pick up the slightest sound from a distance of twenty feet.

'Well, anyway, I suppose we'd better go and tell your Commander-in-Chief this most unfortunate news, straight away.'

'Immediately, I should think,' added Pollock, thinking that the sooner his President found out that Splotitty was now holding seven people hostage, and would therefore be in a position to have no less than twenty-eight different human appendages pulled off, one after the other, live on intergalactic TV, including those attached to two members of the UKA Space Police, the sooner he might be persuaded to abandon his deranged idea of taking over Titan. But as he thought that one over, knowing his President as well as he did, he knew that it would take a lot more than the public killing of seven people to dissuade him.

However, it was then that Pollock had an idea.

'Could I be so bold as to make a suggestion, Lord Von Splotitty?'

'By all means, please, go ahead.'

'In private, if I may?'

Splotitty looked around at all the various lifeforms surrounding them, and said, 'Of course. Walk with me,' and they ambled along in silence together towards the Nla Aafin's grand palace doors.

As soon as Splotitty felt that they were far enough away from the press not to have their conversation recorded, he said, 'You can talk now without the risk of being overheard.'

'I was just wondering,' began Pollock, 'if it might be possible to encourage the prisoners to admit to something more than just killing a cow?'

'But on Titan the Earth cow is the most sacred animal in the whole of the known universe, the purposeful killing of which is punishable by death! I really don't think that we need another reason to pull their arms and legs off.'

'Yes, of course, but I was thinking that if we could somehow get them to confess to something even worse than the brutal murder of a sacred cow, then we may be able to elicit the support of the other members of the Intergalactic Trade Union.'

'For what purpose?'

'Well, I was thinking that if the Intergalactic Trade Union was to threaten Earth with a trade embargo, then President Müller would have no choice but to hand over the video in exchange for having the prisoners change their confession.'

'But what could the prisoners confess to that would have such an effect?'

'If they admitted that they'd tried to assassinate you, and that they'd done so under the direct order of Dick Müller himself! If they said that, then the ITU would have no choice but to implement an immediate trade embargo on Earth by way of punishment. They'd have to because they'd know that if they didn't, then it would leave the door wide open for any one of their leaders to be assassinated.'

'That's what I've always liked about you, Pollock,' began Splotitty. 'You've always been able to come up with such interesting ideas.'

'Thank you, Lord Von Splotitty. That certainly is very kind of you to say so.'

'The Mammary Clans have a vast number of skills and abilities,' continued Splotitty, in a conversational tone, 'far more so than any other species, but an active imagination has never been one of them. Why don't you accompany me inside my palace? I keep it fully oxygenated, so you'll be able to take your helmet off, and we'd then be able to have a chat to my Head of Communications to see how he's getting along with our other special guests.'

CHAPTER TWENTY SIX

HAVING MADE their way into the palace's Communications Room, which was very similar to the room behind the wall of the Lincoln Bedroom back at the White House in that it was a soundproof recording studio with a glass partition that looked out to another room beyond, Lord Von Splotitty said, 'Ah, there you are, General!' as he ushered Pollock inside. 'I'd like to introduce you to the Vice President of Earth, Mr Samuel Pollock.'

The senior Mammary Clan bowed from where he stood behind the mixing desk, as Splotitty continued.

'General Oblama here is our Head of Communications.'

'It's a pleasure to meet you,' said Pollock, who was feeling better for not having to wear his air-helmet.

'Likewise,' said the Head of Communications.

'Oblama oversees all of our broadcasting, programme content, interrogation and torture, isn't that right?'

'That's correct, Olanla Re,' said the pudding-shaped lifeform who, like Field Marshal Ofeefee, was wearing a khaki green toga and a green beret. 'But I also look after light entertainment as well.'

'I thought that came under interrogation and

torture?' asked Splotitty.

Unwilling to contradict his Commander-in-Chief, especially in front of a human being, the General said, 'It does, of course, Olanla Re, but we produce programme content for the women and children as well who, for some strange reason, don't seem to enjoy watching humans having their arms and legs pulled off.'

'Yes, that is strange,' agreed Splotitty, before turning to Pollock. 'As you can no doubt tell, we're very fortunate that the General here is another fluent English speaker, like me, which was one of the reasons I gave him such an important job. Isn't that right, Oblama?'

'Indeed it is, Olanla Re,' said the General.

'Oh, and by the way,' continued Splotitty, looking back at Pollock, 'Olanla Re means "Your Excellency" in Titanese, so if you could call me that, I'd appreciate it.'

'Yes, of course, Your Excellency,' said Pollock, bowing in dutiful reverence as he did.

'Er, no. I'd like you to call me Olanla Re, not Your Excellency!'

'Oh, of course. Sorry! My mistake, Olanla Re.'

'That's better.'

Returning to his Head of Communications, Splotitty asked, 'So, General, how are we getting along with those human prisoners?'

'Well, I suppose we're making progress, Olanla Re,' he said, turning to stare out through the glass partition.

There, facing them, still wearing their gravity-coats but without their air-helmets on, were Inspector Capstan, Lieutenant Dewbush, Lucy Butterbum, and the three members of the Intergalactic Free Rangers. They were sitting on chairs that Titan's Communications Department had kept in storage for just such occasions, with their hands tied behind their backs and gags over their mouths, and covered in some sort of white powder.

'Ah! There they are!' exclaimed Splotitty, 'I've never seen so many dangerous-looking assassins in all my life, don't you think, Mr Vice President?'

'I completely agree with you, Olanla Re,' replied Pollock.

'And what have you found out from them so far, General?'

'Not a huge amount as yet, but we don't believe them to be assassins, Olanla Re.'

'Oh, I think you'll find that they *are* assassins, wouldn't you say, Mr Vice President?'

'Most definitely, Olanla Re.'

'I also think you'll find that they were sent here to assassinate me. And by non-other than the President of Earth himself! Isn't that right, Mr Vice President?'

'I'm afraid that is also correct, Olanla Re.'

194

'Then you seem to know more than I do, Olanla Re,' said the General, with another graceful effort at a bow. 'Unfortunately, all we've managed to find out so far is what their favourite colours are, if they're married or single, and what they do for a living.'

'Is that all?' asked Splotitty, clearly not impressed.

'I'm afraid so, Olanla Re. They may just be human beings, but they're proving to have a remarkable high tolerance to pain. None of them have so far said a word.'

'Then how did you find out what all their favourite colours were?'

'Ah, well; you see those two on the end?' he asked, pointing at Detective Inspector Capstan and Lieutenant Dewbush.

'The one with the big nose and the younger-looking one?'

'Yes, those two. Well, they're from the UKA Space Police, and inside their suit jacket pockets we found these two pairs of glasses.'

'And?' asked Splotitty, looking down at them. 'So what?'

'We had to break them in half to find out but when you look through the lenses they tell you lots of very useful information about whatever it is that you look at. Would you like to have a go, Olanla Re?' and the general offered him one half of a pair.

Taking it from him, Splotitty positioned the lens in

195

such a way that he could peer through it with one of his four eyes.

'Well I never!' he exclaimed, moments later. 'You're right, General! All the information just seems to appear directly above their heads!'

'Remarkable, isn't it?'

'Yes, quite remarkable! And I suggest that as soon as we've persuaded them to talk, we ask them how these work, so that we can make some for ourselves.'

'What an excellent idea, Olanla Re.'

'But that still doesn't help us to make them say what we want them to say, does it?' Splotitty pointed out, as he took the glass down from his eye and examined it in his tentacles.

'Unfortunately not, Olanla Re.'

Turning to Pollock, Splotitty asked, 'Mr Vice President, I don't suppose you have any ideas as to how we could make the human prisoners a little more communicative?'

'Um,' began Pollock, and looking at the General, asked, 'May I enquire what you've tried so far?'

'Oh, just about everything, really. First we made them stand in a bucket of salt, but to no effect. Then we submerged their hand things in salt, but again nothing. After that we played ultra-high frequency sound at them over the speaker system, but even when it was turned up to maximum it just didn't seem to have any effect. So then we tied down their arms and

196

poured salt over them, but again nothing, and then, as a last resort, we poured an entire bucket of salt over their heads!'

On hearing that, Splotitty winced.

'And that didn't work?' he asked, with some amazement.

'Regrettably not, Olanla Re.'

'These humans certainly do seem to have nuts that are difficult to crack.'

Pollock was about to correct Splotitty's English phraseology again when he changed his mind and instead looked at the General and asked, 'Am I correct in assuming that you've never interrogated a human before?'

'I must admit that this is the first time we've bothered to ask them any questions. We normally just film them having their arms and legs pulled off before feasting on their internal organs.'

Up until that moment, Pollock hadn't known that if they did decide to pull his arms and legs off, they'd be dining on his internal organs afterwards, and swallowed down some whisky milkshake-flavoured vomit that had just arrived uninvited into his mouth.

Meanwhile, Splotitty turned to ask him, 'I don't suppose you have any ideas that could maybe help us, Mr Vice President?'

'Oh, er, yes! I'm sure I do,' he said, even more determined to make himself useful.

'Then please, we all have ears.'

'It's actually, "we're all ears" but that aside, I'd suggest you start by getting hold of some tools, like pliers, or something.'

'Pliers?' asked the General.

'Well, not pliers, necessarily. A hacksaw would do the trick.'

'A hacksaw?'

'An axe, then?'

'An axe?'

'How about a chisel?'

'A what?'

'A screwdriver?'

'Er…?

'OK, what about knives and forks?'

'Ah! Knives and forks! Yes, I've heard of them, but sadly no. Unfortunately we only ever use spoons to eat.'

'You have nothing on Titan that's sharp and made of stainless steel?'

'Sharp?'

'You know, something pointy?'

'Pointy?'

'Never mind. We'll have to think of something else,' and Pollock folded his arms and massaged his chin for a moment as he stared up at the ceiling. But it didn't take him long to come up with an idea, and asked, 'Do you think it would be possible for me to speak to the prisoners?'

The General looked over at his Commander-in-Chief. 'Would that be acceptable, Olanla Re?'

'I can't see what harm it would do,' replied Splotitty.

Having been granted permission, the General said to Earth's Vice President, 'If you press this button here, and speak into this microphone, then they'll be able to hear you, but if you want to hear them talk, then we'd better take their gags off.'

'That might not be necessary, General,' said Pollock. 'Can you film them whilst I'm talking to them?'

'Certainly,' and as the general pressed another button, he moved to one side and said, 'It's recording now for you.'

Stepping over to the desk, Pollock said, 'Thank you,' before pressing down the microphone's button and saying, 'Hello, everyone. Are you having a good time?'

The six prisoners sitting down before him all began shaking their heads with some vigour, as a clear indication that they weren't.

'That's nice. Now, I'd like all those of you who wouldn't, I repeat *wouldn't* like to have their arms and legs pulled off live on intergalactic TV to put your hands up.'

As Pollock stood back from the microphone,

Splotitty, the general and himself enjoyed watching as the six people all desperately tried to raise their hands. But as they were tied firmly behind their backs, none were able to.

Re-approaching the microphone, Pollock said, 'So you're all saying that you *would* like to have your arms and legs pulled off?'

Now the six people started shaking their heads, but with even more vigour this time.

'Then I'm sorry, but we are going to need to see a show of hands.'

But none of them obliged, so Pollock said, 'I promise you that it will be even harder to raise your hands once your arms have been pulled off.'

Still nobody moved.

'I must admit that I am a little surprised. I'd have thought you'd have all been rather keen *not* to have your arms and legs pulled off, being that it's probably the most painful way for a human to die.'

He paused for a moment, before saying, 'I suppose it could be a communications problem, being that you've all got gags on. Tell you what, let's try asking you something else. All those who are not, I repeat *not* human, please raise your hands?'

Unsurprisingly, none of them did.

'So you're human then?' asked Pollock, and they all began nodding.

'OK, now, keep your hands down if you didn't, I

repeat *didn't* deliberately murder a sacred cow?'

Once again, they all kept their hands down as they began exchanging relieved glances with each other.

'Excellent!' said Pollock. 'I really think we're making progress. Now, I just have one final question after which we should be able to let you go. Keep your hands down if you were, I repeat *were* sent here by the President of Earth, Dick Müller IV, to assassinate the Supreme High Councillor of Titan and Commander in Chief of the Mammary Clans, Lord Von Splotitty?'

Despite doing their absolute very best to raise them, once again their hands remained firmly behind their backs.

'Thank you, gentlemen, and lady of course. You've been most helpful,' and with that he turned back to face first Titan's Head of Communications and then the Supreme High Councillor of Titan and Commander-in-Chief of the Mammary Clans, who by then were both staring at him as if he was a living god, sent down from heaven itself to teach them advanced methods of interrogation, and asked, 'Do you think that would be enough to convince the Intergalactic Trade Union, or should I see what I can do with a spoon?'

'It would appear, Mr Vice President,' said Lord Von Splotitty, 'that you are a human of many talents.'

'You are most kind, Olanla Re,' said Pollock, and bowed once more.

'I suggest we all make our way to my private rooms for a celebratory milkshake, and from where we'll be able to give your Earth President a call with the happy news that we have in our custardy no less than six human beings who have just confessed to having tried to assassinate me under his direct orders. Now that will be a turn-up for his books!' and with that he opened up his gaping wide mouth and let out a jolly sort of laugh, and with Pollock and the General feeling obliged to join in, they followed Splotitty out to make the call together.

CHAPTER TWENTY SEVEN

INSIDE THE interrogation room, Capstan, Dewbush, Lucy and the Intergalactic Free Rangers sat staring at the one human and two more local-looking lifeforms behind the screen, stunned by the fact that one minute they thought they were going to be cleared of all charges and released scot-free, only to find the very next that they'd just confessed to being the President of Earth's personal assassins, sent to kill none other than Lord Von Splotitty himself, something they felt they'd be unlikely to get away with.

They watched their interrogators having a jolly good laugh about the whole thing as they made their way out, and the six prisoners found themselves alone.

In a state of desperation, they began bouncing up and down on their chairs, pretty much at the same time, in a rather sad attempt to free themselves from what was probably going to be certain death. And although liberty evaded them, Dewbush did at least manage to move his mouth in such a way that he was able to wriggle the gag down onto his chin, allowing him to speak.

'I can talk, sir!' he declared, with obvious delight.

'Ell ung, ewush,' said Capstan. He'd meant to say, 'Well done, Dewbush,' in a sarcastic tone, as he really couldn't see the benefit of suddenly having re-discovered the gift of speech when they'd already confessed to being assassins, but it was nearly impossible to say anything with the gag tied around his mouth, and certainly not something that could be easily recognised as sarcasm.

Then Dewbush said, 'I'm going to try to move my chair over towards you, sir. Then I might be able to take your gag off as well, using my mouth!'

However, to Capstan that just sounded like Dewbush was heading his way to give him a snog, and the idea of having his Lieutenant kiss him at any time, let alone in front of four other people, wasn't an appealing prospect. So he attempted to say, 'That really won't be necessary, Dewbush,' but as he still had the gag on it came out as, 'Ack eely onck ee essesseey, euush.'

Unable to understand, Dewbush instead came to the conclusion that his boss had become desperate to talk, so he re-doubled his efforts. With his chair now bouncing up and down at quite a pace, it wasn't long before he was just inches away from Capstan's face.

Capstan attempted to say, 'Honestly, Dewbush, I'm fine. If anything I'd rather you tried to untie my hands,' but it just came out as unintelligible gibberish.

Still not having a clue what his boss was going on about, and after shifting his chair another inch closer, Dewbush was able to grab Capstan's gag with his lips.

With his subordinate's mouth now touching his own, Capstan tried one more time to dissuade him by saying, 'Please stop, Dewbush, I beg you!'

Catching his breath, Dewbush said, 'Don't worry, sir. I've nearly freed your mouth. You'll be able to talk very soon, sir, I promise!'

'That's great, Dewbush. I just can't wait for you to start snogging me again,' said Capstan, with a heavy layer of sarcasm that he knew Dewbush would never have been able to pick up on being as he could hardly understand what he'd just said himself. Besides, Dewbush had already re-attached his mouth to Capstan's, and was already pulling and tugging at the gag with both his teeth and tongue, like a dog trying to pry a sausage from out of its owner's mouth.

Moments later, Dewbush announced, 'I've done it, sir! Your gag's off! You can talk now, sir!'

But all Capstan wanted to do was wipe Dewbush's saliva from his mouth with his sleeve, and with that in mind said, 'I appreciate that, Dewbush. Really, I do. But is there any chance you could do something that could potentially benefit our current predicament?'

'What did you have in mind, sir?'

'Well, instead of spending half an hour trying to get your tongue down my throat, couldn't you have tried untying my hands instead?'

'Your hands, sir?'

'Yes, hands, Dewbush. You remember? They're

usually found on the end of arms, and mine are currently tied behind my back.'

'Oh, I see what you mean, sir. Hold on, I'll see what I can do.'

Dewbush started bouncing up and down on his chair again, until he was able to position it in such a way that he was facing Capstan's back, and by leaning all the way forward could just about reach the rope with his teeth.

But when Capstan felt Dewbush start to lick his hands, in much the same way as he'd been doing to his mouth, and knowing that his Lieutenant's face must be almost up against his backside, he was having second thoughts.

'Nearly done it, sir!' announced Dewbush, before re-engaging the rope with his teeth, lips and tongue.

'Well done, Dewbush, but if you could try not to keep licking my hands, I'd really appreciate it.'

'I'll do my best, sir,' and within another thirty seconds, Capstan's hands were free.

Jumping to his feet, Capstan wasted no more time in wiping his mouth with the backs of both sleeves.

Feeling slightly better, he looked along the line of people still in their chairs, all now staring up at him like a line of puppies desperate to be taken for a walk so they could go to the toilet.

'Right,' he started, and after glancing back over at the recording studio to make sure that it was still empty, went on, 'I'm going to try and untie you.'

'Great idea, sir!' said Dewbush, and as the other four began nodding their approval, Capstan first knelt down behind Dewbush and untied his hands. Then the two of them worked together to untie the hands of Lucy and the three Intergalactic Free Rangers, until all six of them were free.

As soon as Lucy had taken her gag off, she looked at Capstan and asked, 'What's your plan?'

Capstan's only plan so far had been to stop Dewbush from giving him something that, if it wasn't classed as a French kiss, was at least a Belgian one. After he'd failed at doing that, he'd been focussed on getting his arms free so that he could wipe Dewbush's disgusting saliva off his mouth. He'd not had a chance to think beyond that. From what he'd seen of the place on his way in, he certainly had no idea as to how they could escape from a fortress populated by numerous stupid-looking pint-sized Mr Blobby-type creatures, half of which seemed to have been carrying guns which all looked as if they could take down a charging bull elephant from two miles away.

'I think all we'd need to do, sir,' began Dewbush, 'is to sneak out, find a spaceship and get back to Earth.'

'You're right, Dewbush! Now why didn't I think of that?'

'I don't know, sir, but probably because you've never been off-planet before.'

'And do you have any idea just exactly how we're going to sneak out, find a spaceship and get back to Earth, Dewbush?'

'Well, sir, there's a door over there which hasn't been closed properly. And I saw loads of signs on the way in that had all been translated into English, so it shouldn't be too difficult to find our way out. And I also remember passing an armoury on the way in, so if we get back to it we could probably get hold of some guns and then make our way out to the space pad where we landed, sir.'

Capstan narrowed his eyes at his Lieutenant, but Dewbush didn't have that smug expression normally associated with someone who was deliberately showing off, so he simply said, 'Right. Here's the plan. We make our way through that door there and locate the armoury we passed on the way in. Hopefully we'll find some guns there for us to use. We'll then follow the signs out to the space pad, sneak on board the nearest spaceship and make our way back to Earth. Any questions?'

Lucy raised her hand.

'Yes, Lucy?'

'We're going to have to rescue the cow as well. We can't leave her behind.'

She was right. Capstan's orders had been to find and return both Lucy Butterbum *and* the stolen cow. Fortunately, however, he'd only been ordered to find

208

and return one cow, and so shouldn't get into trouble for leaving the dead one behind.

'OK, here's the *new* plan,' he began. 'We make our way through that door there and locate the armoury we passed on the way in. Hopefully we'll find some guns there for us to use. We'll then follow the signs out to the space pad, sneak on board the nearest spaceship, fly back to where we last saw the cow, hope to God it's still there, load it on board and make our way back to Earth. Any questions?'

None of them did, so Capstan said, 'Right, follow me!' and they scurried over towards the door which, as Dewbush had correctly pointed out, someone had forgotten to close.

CHAPTER TWENTY EIGHT

ONCE LORD VON SPLOTITTY, Vice President Pollock and General Oblama had been welcomed by Splotitty's wife into their private quarters, and after she'd made them all a special strawberry banana chocolate raspberry and vanilla milkshake before being ordered to leave, Splotitty said, 'I think a toast is in order, don't you?'

'Absolutely,' agreed Pollock, even though he still had a hangover and the idea of drinking any sort of milkshake really didn't appeal, let alone a strawberry banana chocolate raspberry and vanilla one.

As the three of them raised their milkshakes, Splotitty said, 'To me!'

For a split second Pollock thought he was joking, but when General Oblama clinked his glass against Splotitty's and said, 'To you, Olanla Re!' he realised he wasn't, and joined the General in clinking his glass with the others whilst repeating, 'To you, Olanla Re!'

Once Splotitty and the General drained their glasses and burped their appreciation, and after Pollock took a sip from his and then did his best not to throw it straight up again, Splotitty said, 'Right! Time to call Earth, don't you think?'

Pressing a purple button on the desk they were

standing besides, he leaned in and said, 'Ṣe o gba Aare ti Earth, Dick Müller, lori foonu fun mi jọwọ?'

Like the last time Splotitty had called President Müller, when they were on board his starship, a voice came straight back over the intercom, saying, 'Otun kuro, Olanla Re.' But unlike the last time, they had to wait a little longer for him to come on the line, presumably because he wasn't behind his desk, waiting for the call. But it wasn't long before he did.

'Hello, Timmy! And how are you today?'

Splotitty stared at Pollock. He'd forgotten to ask him why the President of Earth kept calling him Timmy all the time, and made a mental note to do so as soon as the call was over.

'Very well, thank you, President Müller. And yourself?'

'All the better for hearing from you, Timmy my boy!'

'That's nice,' said Splotitty.

'I must say, Timmy, that I'm certainly pleased you called. I'd nearly given up on you, and was just about to send that video of you and those girls over to the Intergalactic News Federation.'

'Ah yes, and that was precisely why I was calling, President Müller.'

'Oh good! So when are you going to hand Titan over to me?'

'Well…'

'It's just that I can't wait to tell Congress that I was able to persuade you to. I've even decided on a name for it: "The United Tits of America"! What do you think? It's not very imaginative, I know, but it works well within the rest of my portfolio.'

'And that's what I wanted to talk to you about, President Müller.'

'Good, good. So when are you making the announcement that it's mine?'

'Just as soon as you've been able to tell me why you sent six of your human beings over to Titan to assassinate me?'

There was a pause on the other end of the line.

While President Müller was presumably thinking that one over, Lord Von Splotitty, Vice President Pollock and General Oblama all started winking at each other, with a varying number of eyes.

It wasn't long before President Müller came back on, saying, 'To be honest Timmy, I don't recall sending anyone over to assassinate you, which is odd, as it's the sort of thing I'd normally remember.'

'Oh, I can assure you that you did, President Müller. There are six of them, they're all sitting in our recording studio as we speak, and I have them on video saying that they were sent here by you to assassinate me.'

There was no response from Müller, so Splotitty

went on, 'Now I don't know about you, President Müller, but I'm fairly sure that the Intergalactic Trade Union won't be too pleased to hear that one celestial body leader had attempted to take the life of another celestial body leader. I believe it goes against the ITU Trading Agreement, the one which we've all signed. And I suspect that should they find out that you did try to have me assassinated they'll do one of two things. Either they'll place a trading embargo on you that will in all likelihood cripple your economy, or, worse still, they'll kick you out and you'll have to go back to fending for yourself, just like you had to before we were kind enough to go out of our way to discover you.'

Still there was silence from the end of the line, and it went on for so long that Splotitty eventually asked, 'Are you still there, President Müller?'

'Yes, sorry, Timmy. I'm still here. My wife was just asking if I'd like a coffee. What were you saying again?'

Splotitty sighed.

'I was saying that if you don't send me the original recording you took of me from last night, and any copies you may have, then I'm going to send the recording I have of the six assassins straight over to the ITU.'

'And that's what you said before, was it?' asked Müller.

'Well, no, but it's what I'm saying now.'

213

'Right, I see.' They then heard him say, 'Oh, thanks, Darling, that looks just perfect,' before he continued, 'Sorry about that. So you're saying that you have a video of six people from Earth who've actually said, out loud, that I sent them over there to assassinate you?'

'They didn't actually say it, but they've admitted to it, yes!'

'I see,' and they all clearly heard him stirring what they assumed to be the coffee his wife had just made for him. 'So, if they didn't actually say that I sent them over there to assassinate you, how was it possible for them to have admitted to it?'

'Ah, well, when we asked them to put their hands down if you'd sent them over to assassinate me, they all did!'

President Müller could be heard taking a sip from his coffee, before he asked, 'And I assume that was because they were all gagged and had their hands tied behind their backs before you asked them?'

'That's as maybe, but it's not the point! They've all confessed, and we have them on video doing so, and if you don't send me the video you took of me from last night, I'm sending the one which has our prisoners' confession straight over to the ITU!'

They heard Müller take another sip from his coffee before he said, 'I'm sorry, Timmy, but it's not going to work, I'm afraid.'

'And why's that, may I ask?'

'Taking someone prisoner, gagging them, tying their hands behind their back, and then asking them to either raise or lower their hands in response to a series of incriminating questions simply isn't admissible in the Intergalactic Courts. I think you'll find that they have to actually say that they did something, out loud. And even then they have to do so of their own free will, and not after they've just been tortured. Sorry about that.'

But Splotitty wasn't going to be defeated quite so easily.

'Then we'll simply go back to them, take their gags off and try again! It will only be a matter of time before we get them to tell us whatever it is that we need.'

'And you really have these so-called "assassins" in your custody, do you?' asked Müller, who didn't sound convinced by the whole thing, although he did sound as if he'd just started eating a biscuit.

'Yes, of course we have the assassins in our custardy!' said Splotitty, clearly becoming a little irritated. 'Why would we be saying all this if we didn't have them in our custardy?'

'I've no idea, Timmy, but it does all sound like a bit of a coincidence. You know, me getting a video of you doing some frankly rather disgusting things to some of our youngest and most innocent girls, just as you've

215

managed to dig up six so-called "assassins" who I allegedly sent over to kill you.'

'Then I'd better show them to you, hadn't I?'

'It would be a start, I suppose,' said Müller. 'Anyway, call me back when you can, preferably with them all saying that I sent them to kill you, out loud, and we can speak more about it then,' and with that he ended the call.

Splotitty immediately turned to General Oblama to ask, 'Is it possible to have a live video of the prisoners transmitted to Earth so that President Müller can see it whilst I'm talking to him?'

'It should be, Olanla Re. I'll give my technical assistant a call. I'm sure he'll be able to sort something out.' General Oblama then leaned over the same desk, pressed the purple button again, and said, 'Gba Golag fun mi, bayi!'

Leading Vice President Pollock away, Splotitty asked, 'Can human beings be made to confess to something they didn't actually do without having to torture them first?'

'Probably not, Olanla Re,' Pollock replied. 'But what you can do is torture them when they're not being filmed, and then turn the cameras back on when they're ready to talk. As long as there are no visible signs on their faces that they've been tortured, I'm sure the Intergalactic Courts would be able to accept that as admissible evidence.'

'OK, great! Can I leave you to sort that out?'

With a broad grin, Pollock bowed, saying, 'It would be my absolute pleasure, Olanla Re.'

But his smile wasn't to last long, as General Oblama came waddling up behind them with a worried look.

'I have some very bad news, Olanla Re. It would appear that the prisoners have escaped!'

'Escaped?'

'I'm afraid so, Olanla Re'

'But—how could they have escaped?'

'I'm not sure, Olanla Re. But they're not where we left them.'

'Right! Sound the alarm, General! I want those prisoners found, brought back to the studio and made to say out loud that they're assassins sent to kill me by the President of Earth. And if you can't, then it'll be *you* who's tied to a chair having buckets of salt poured over your head. Do you understand?'

'Fully, Olanla Re,' and gave a quick bow before wobbling his way back to the desk, just as fast as his pudding-shaped body would allow, where there was a large red button with the word ITANIJI in capitals over the top and ALARM written underneath. He slapped it hard with one of his tentacles, and the sound of an enormous ice cream van began chiming throughout the palace and the grounds beyond.

CHAPTER TWENTY NINE

AFTER CAPSTAN had poked his head out of the recording studio to make sure the coast was clear, Dewbush, Lucy and the three Intergalactic Free Rangers followed him out into the corridor beyond. And with Dewbush's helpful guidance, and the various signs on the walls, it didn't take them long to find their way back to the room they'd passed on the way in, the one that had Ihamora written on the door with its English translation of Armoury displayed below.

'So far so good,' whispered Capstan.

'At least it doesn't seem to be as busy as it was when we came in, sir,' commented Dewbush, who was a little surprised that they hadn't yet run into any Mammary Clans.

'It's probably their lunchbreak,' said Lucy, feeling hungry.

But as Capstan grabbed the door's handle their luck seemed to have run out.

'It's locked!' he called out behind him.

'Are you sure, sir?'

'Of course I'm sure, Dewbush!' said Capstan, as he cupped both hands over his eyes in an effort to peer through the door's circular window.

'Did you turn the handle clockwise or anti-clockwise, sir?'

'I've no idea, Dewbush. Does it matter?'

'It's just that door handles on Titan open anti-clockwise, sir. Unlike most humans, the Mammary Clans are left-handed.'

'Frankly, Dewbush, I really don't see how Mammary Clans being left or right handed has anything to do with the door being locked, especially when they don't even have hands!'

'And they're also not known for locking things, sir,' continued Dewbush, as if he wasn't listening to what his boss was saying, 'which is why they have such a low crime rate.'

But if Dewbush wasn't listening to Capstan, Capstan had still been listening to Dewbush, and that last comment definitely caught his attention.

'Sorry, Dewbush, I assume you meant to say that they don't have to lock anything *because* they have a low crime rate?'

'Er, no sir. It's the other way round.'

'The other way round?' repeated Capstan.

'Yes, sir. It's known as double-reverse criminal psychology. It's been proven that people only consider something worth stealing if it's locked up. If it's not, then it's unlikely that anyone would be bothered to steal it. That's why these days most planetary systems actively discourage anyone from locking anything up, and because Titan's one of them, it's unlikely that the door is locked, sir.'

Capstan shook his head in a bid to understand what his subordinate had just said, but it made no sense whatsoever, especially to a 21st Century policeman. However, considering their current predicament, in which they were attempting to escape from a fate that many would consider to be worse than death, he was keen not to have to discuss the matter anymore than they already had. So instead of doing so, he tried turning the door handle the other way.

'It's not locked,' he said, a moment later, feeling both a bit stupid and a little upset that his subordinate had been proven right. However, putting his own personal feelings to one side, the door was now open, so he led everyone in.

Inside they found themselves in a predominately white room with walls lined with identical black Nerf gun-type weapons.

'Does anyone know how to use these?' asked Capstan, gazing around at them all.

'I do, sir,' said Dewbush, and he stepped forward to take one off the wall. 'They're the MDK 16mm Exterminator, sir, which is basically the larger version of our MDK 12mm Decapitators. They must have a trade agreement with Earth to buy them from us.'

That didn't help any of the rest of them to understand how they worked, so looking around at them, Dewbush added, 'Basically you just point and shoot.'

That was enough for Capstan.

'Right, everyone grab a gun. But just make sure you keep them pointed at the ground, especially if you're standing behind me! If I find that someone's blown my head off, I won't be too pleased, I can assure you!'

'I don't think you'd know if someone has blown your head off, sir, especially if they'd done so from behind. They'd need to be standing in front of you for that to happen, although, saying that, if they were standing behind you, and they said that they were about to blow your head off, then you probably would know about it then, sir.'

'That's fascinating, Lieutenant, but either way I'd really prefer it if nobody blew my head off, so if you could all keep your guns facing down, I'd be very grateful!'

'But what if someone's about to shoot us, sir?' asked Dewbush, 'and we need to shoot back?'

He'd raised a good point, and after thinking about it for a few moments, Capstan said, 'If that happens, then I suggest you make sure you're standing in front of me before you start shooting.'

'Good idea, sir!' said Dewbush, and for once Capstan had to agree with him. His suggestion *was* a good idea! Not only would it prevent that person from shooting him in the back, but it would also help to shield him from being shot by the person shooting at them.

'Right, are you ready?' asked Capstan, looking around at everyone as they all nodded back at him. 'OK. Let's go!' and he turned back to the door. But the moment he re-opened it, Capstan nearly walked straight into a larger-than-average Mammary Clan, with two others standing right behind him who, perhaps unsurprisingly, looked just as surprised to see six human beings inside their armoury as Capstan looked to see them.

It was at that moment the alarm went off, and as the sound of a giant ice cream van reverberated around their ears, the three Mammary Clans stared around at each other before the front one said, 'O ti wa ni itaniji. Je ki a gba kuro lati nibi!' and they wobbled off down the corridor, leaving Capstan and the others breathing a sigh of relief.

'Does anyone know what they said?' asked Capstan, out of curiosity.

Calisto thought for a moment before saying, 'I think they said, "It's the alarm. Let's get out of here".'

'Fair enough,' said Capstan.

'It must be just a general alarm, sir,' Dewbush said. 'Not one specifically relating to escaping prisoners.'

'That makes sense, I suppose,' said Capstan. 'Anyway,' he continued, 'I suggest we don't hang around waiting to see if they come back,' and with that he poked his head out the door again, and seeing the coast now clear, led the way back out into the corridor.

There he stopped and asked, 'Which way, Dewbush?'

'If Calisto was right, sir, and they did say, "Let's get out of here," then I think there's a fair chance that they are indeed "getting out of here". And as that's what we're trying to do as well, it may be a good idea to follow them, sir.'

Although he'd taken a while to say it, for once Capstan thought Dewbush had said something that made remarkable good sense, and so the six of them started almost running down the corridor, in the same direction that the three Mammary Clans had taken.

It wasn't long before Dewbush called out, 'I think that's them up ahead, sir.'

'I think you're right, Dewbush,' said Capstan, and about thirty seconds later, the six of them overtook the three Mammary Clans, all on their way out of the building, prompting Capstan to say, 'They can't run very fast, can they?'

'It's because their feet are biologically the same as slugs and snails, sir, apart from the fact that they have two of them instead of one.'

As interesting as that was, Capstan was more focussed on finding his way out, preferably to where they kept all the spaceships, so he didn't bother to say anything in response.

It wasn't long before they reached a wide double-door, each with two round windows and one with a sign that again had been translated into English that said Space Port.

Reaching it, Capstan signalled for everyone to get down, so that their heads were below the two windows. He then lifted his up so that he could peer through the closest one.

'There are loads of Mammary Clans out there,' he said, a moment or two later.

'What are they doing, sir?' asked Dewbush.

'They just seem to be lining up, and there's another one counting them all. They must have thought the alarm was a fire drill.'

'Maybe it was, sir,' said Dewbush.

'There are loads of spaceships out there as well,' added Capstan, as he continued to stare out through the door's window. 'Any idea which one we should go for?'

'Unfortunately, sir, I've just realised something rather important.'

'What's that, Lieutenant?' asked Capstan.

By way of an answer, Dewbush pointed at one of the signs on the door, the one that had a red circle with O2 written in the middle, crossed out by a single red line.

They still had their gravity-coats on but they'd all forgotten that they'd also need their air-helmets to breathe beyond the palace walls.

'Well, that's that then,' said Capstan. He didn't consider himself to be the sort of person who would give up easily, but he was exactly the sort of person who would give up easily.

Dewbush joined him by the doors to take a look out the window for himself.

'I think we can still make it, sir,' he said, with an optimistic tone.

'And how'd you work that one out?' asked Capstan.

'That's Lord Von Splotitty's starship over there, sir. The big pink one.'

'Yes, and?'

'Well, sir, it's well known that he keeps it oxygenated, just like his palace. He believes oxygen has certain health benefits, sir.'

'I'd have to agree with him on that one,' said Capstan.

'So if we simply hold our breath and make a run for it, sir, we should be OK.'

'If we hold our breath and make a run for it?' repeated Capstan, staring at his subordinate.

'That's right, sir. Once we're on board, we should be able to breathe.'

'It's a brilliant plan, Dewbush, no, really it is, apart from one tiny little detail.'

'What's that, sir?'

'If we reach the spaceship and it doesn't have an oxygen supply, then we'll die!'

'Well, yes, sir. It's a bit of a risk, I suppose. But if we get there and there is no air, then we might be able to find a way to turn it on, sir.'

'Having just run over to the ship, whilst holding our breath?'

'Yes, sir.'

Capstan wasn't even vaguely convinced, and turned back to the others to ask, 'What do you think? Lucy?'

'Well, if it's a choice between dying of asphyxiation, or staying here and having our arms and legs pulled off, then I'd probably go with asphyxiation.'

'Everyone else?' asked Capstan, as he looked around at the others.

But they all seemed to be in agreement with Lucy.

'I suppose one of us could go first,' suggested Dewbush. 'To see if it does have oxygen on board, sir?'

It was another good idea, but this one came with a very obvious caveat, and although they all knew what that was, none of them particularly wanted to say it out loud.

Eventually, Dewbush said, 'I'll go, sir! I don't mind.'

'You don't mind?' asked Capstan, unable to work out if he was incredibly brave or just so stupid that he didn't realise what would happen to him if he arrived on board the starship and there was no air for him to breathe.

'Well, I suppose I'd mind if it doesn't have oxygen on board, sir, and I can't find a way to turn it on.'

He was being brave then, thought Capstan, as he stared at his still relatively new subordinate. But it was no use. As much as he really didn't want to, and he *really* didn't want to, Capstan was the senior officer, and he knew that it was for him to go before anyone else did.

'That's commendable of you, Lieutenant, but I believe it's my job to go first. After all, I am the oldest, and by about four hundred and fifty years.'

Lucy and the three Intergalactic Free Rangers stared at him, in both awe of his bravery and because he didn't look anywhere near four hundred and fifty years old, even by modern day standards.

Sensing what they were thinking, Dewbush explained to them, 'Detective Inspector Capstan is from the 21st Century. He was cryogenically frozen and was only woken up about two days ago.'

That did explain a lot, and Lucy and the others began nodding their understanding, and then just crouched there, waiting for him to go.

Peering out the window, Dewbush gave his boss a little prompt. 'The coast is clear, sir.'

'Right then,' said Capstan. 'So I just hold my breath, run up the ramp, and then I should be able to breathe?'

'That's right Sir, but if you can't, have a look around for either a lever or a dial next to a sign with

O2 written on it.'

'OK. I suppose I'd better go then.'

'I think so, sir. Yes.'

'And there's absolutely no alternative?'

'None that I can think of, sir.'

'OK,' he repeated, and after taking one last look through the window, he breathed in and out a few times, during which time everyone gave him an encouraging smile as they held both their thumbs up.

Returning the thumbs up signal, he nodded for possibly the last time at Dewbush, pushed open the door and began a gentle jog over towards the huge pink starship that was about two hundred yards away.

As soon as he'd gone, Dewbush pulled the door closed, and after watching him for a few moments through the window, said, 'I've just thought of an alternative.'

'What's that?' asked Lucy.

'We could have gone back to find our air-helmets before we left. I'd forgotten about those,' and was about to call his boss back when he realised he'd almost reached the starship he was heading for.

CHAPTER THIRTY

CAPSTAN JOGGED up the ramp into what seemed to be a deserted starship, and it was only then that he realised he had another problem; not whether or not there was oxygen on board, but just how exactly he was going to find out if there was, or wasn't. He looked desperately around for some sort of a gauge, or maybe a sign that was lit up with O2 written on it, and not being able to see one, he came to the realisation that there was only one way to find out, and that was to do what he was becoming increasingly desperate to do.

Thank God for that, he thought, about five seconds later as he began to take in great lungfuls of what fortunately was real-life fully-oxygenated air.

Once he'd caught his breath he held it again to walk back down the ramp. There he crouched low so that his brothers in arms, and legs, could see him, and gave them a good solid thumbs-up. And as soon as he saw Dewbush return the signal and pushed the double doors open for them all to begin jogging their way over towards him, he ducked back inside the ship, breathed again, and had a look around, preferably for a sign that said Cockpit This Way, or something similar. But he couldn't see one, so he thought he'd better wait for his subordinate, who seemed to have a natural ability for finding his way around alien-type places, like restaurants, palaces and, hopefully, a large pink starship.

Dewbush led Lucy and the Intergalactic Free Rangers on board, breathed in, gave Detective Inspector Capstan a beaming great smile and said, 'Well done, sir!' and stepped over to shake him by the hand.

This gesture took Capstan completely by surprise, but after a moment of staring at Dewbush's proffered hand, he came to the conclusion that he probably had done something rather brave after all, even if running into an unmanned starship to simply start breathing in and out didn't, at first, seem particularly so.

As Capstan shook Dewbush's hand with some gusto, Lucy, Starstrider, Calisto and Oberon all stepped forward to do the same.

'Thank you,' said Capstan, magnanimously, 'but we're not out of the woods yet. We need to work out how to get this thing off the ground, back to where we left that cow and then home to Earth, before celebrations are in order, and I can't find a sign for where the cockpit is.'

'It will be near the front, sir,' said Dewbush, and began to lead the way forward.

Once again, luck was on their side as the front of the ship seemed to be just as deserted as the back of it, and by simply heading forward, Dewbush soon stumbled on the relatively small cockpit.

'It's over here, sir,' he called back, and then simply stared at the complex control systems, in much the same way as your average grandmother would stare at a TV's remote control.

When Capstan came in, Dewbush apologised, saying, 'Unfortunately sir, it's a lot different from what I was expecting. I can't see a steering wheel, and there doesn't seem to be a brake or an accelerator either! I'm really not sure I'm going to be able to fly it.'

Lucy and the three Intergalactic Free Rangers joined them, and Starstrider turned to Calisto, the one in charge of driving and navigation to ask, 'What do you think?'

'About what?'

'Can you fly it, dumb ass?'

'Oh, er…' he replied, as he had a quick look around, and after a moment or two said, 'I don't see why not. It looks like it has a similar set up to the YouGet van, just without the seat,' and with that he smiled around at everyone, pleased to be of use.

'Well?' asked Starstrider, after Calisto had finished grinning at them all.

'Well what?'

'Can you start flying it, please?'

'Oh, yes. Sorry, of course,' and Calisto pushed his way forward as he asked, 'I assume we're going back to

82, Skylar Gardens?'

'If that's where you were keeping the cows,' said Lucy, 'then yes!'

'OK, no problem. If you could all find somewhere to sit, it shouldn't take long.'

But as there wasn't a single chair to be found, they all just remained where they were and held on to something, just in case Calisto couldn't fly it as well as he seemed to think he could.

CHAPTER THIRTY ONE

'HAVE YOU FOUND them yet?' asked Lord Von Splotitty, who'd taken to pacing up and down the room like a duck on a hot tin roof.

'Er, not yet, Olanla Re, but we're bound to, very soon!'

Something caught Splotitty's eye out of the window and he stopped to peer out of it, down towards the space port.

'Why are all my guards lined up outside?' he asked.

'They're being counted, Olanla Re.'

'Counted?' repeated Splotitty.

'That is correct, Olanla Re.'

'But why are they being counted?'

'Er…' began his General, 'I think that they're just making sure that they're all there, Olanla Re?'

'But why wouldn't they be all there?'

'Because of the fire, Olanla Re.'

'Fire! What fire?'

'Well, there wasn't *actually* a fire, Olanla Re, but it's just that they thought that the alarm was for one.'

'For one what?'

'For a fire, Olanla Re.'

'Are you seriously telling me that they thought that it was a fire alarm, and they're now all lining up to be counted to make sure everyone's there whilst my six prisoners are probably halfway back to Earth by now?'

'Um, well…' began General Oblama, but didn't think it wise to either confirm or deny that that was what had happened.

'Well, General, it looks like you have a choice, doesn't it?'

'It does, Olanla Re?'

'Either you can find a bucket of salt and stick your head in it, or you can go down there and tell my guards to stop counting each other and start finding my prisoners!'

'Of course, Olanla Re,' and dared to wait a moment before asking, 'I don't suppose I could choose the second option, Olanla Re?'

'JUST GET OUT THERE AND TELL THEM ALL TO START LOOKING FOR MY PRISONERS!'

'Yes, Olanla Re. Right away, Olanla Re.'

While Lord Von Splotitty and General Oblama had what could be best described as a communication problem, Samuel Pollock, Earth's Vice President, had been looking out the same window that Lord Von Splotitty had.

'I hate to interrupt, Olanla Re, but I think I just saw five humans run into the back of your starship.'

'My starship!' He and the General waddled over to take a look for themselves.

'Well, first I saw one human run into it, but I didn't think anything of it, as six of them had escaped. But then I saw another five go in, and realised that if I added the first one to the other five, then that would make the correct number of prisoners you were looking for, Olanla Re.'

'You mean, six?' asked Splotitty.

'Correct, Olanla Re!'

'So what you're basically telling me is that you've managed to work out that five plus one equals six?' asked Splotitty, struggling to believe what he was being forced to listen to.

'Um, well, I suppose so, yes!'

'Is everyone here a complete idiot, or am I the last lifeform in the universe with a fully functioning brain?'

'Er…' began Pollock, unsure as to how to answer that one, but fortunately for him he saw something that he thought would help change the subject, and looking over his shoulder, pointed down and said, 'I think your starship is taking off, Olanla Re.'

Pollock was right, and the three of them watched in stunned silence as Lord Von Splotitty's private starship began to slowly lift itself off the ground.

'General,' began Splotitty, remaining almost unnaturally calm. 'I want my starship back. So may I suggest you tell our star fleet to set off after them?'

'Yes, Olanla Re.'

'But this time, is there any chance you could not do

so by raising the alarm? I don't particularly wish to have to wait for everyone to be lined up and counted again.'

'Of course, Olanla Re.,' and a moment later asked, 'So, should I go and tell them myself, Olanla Re?'

'YES, GO AND TELL THEM YOURSELF, YOU IDIOT!'

CHAPTER THIRTY TWO

'WE SHOULD BE over Skylar Gardens now,' announced Calisto, about half an hour after leaving the Nla Aafin's palace space port.

'Any sign of Daisy?' asked Lucy, standing on her tiptoes in an effort to see over Calisto's head as he began banking the giant pink starship over to the port side.

'She's there alright,' he announced, 'and still surrounded by Mammary Clans!'

Intrigued, Lucy moved all the way to the front to take a look for herself, before reporting back to the others. 'They've put a crown on her head, and a purple robe over her back!'

'I assume they've still kept her oxygen mask on?' asked Starstrider.

'They have, and I suspect the robe is probably a gravity blanket, else she'd have drifted off by now.'

It was then that Calisto announced, 'Unfortunately, it looks like we have a bit of a problem.'

'What's that?' asked Starstrider.

'We're just far too big to land, I'm afraid.'

'That's probably my fault,' said Dewbush. 'I didn't take into consideration the size of the spaceship we'd need in order to rescue the cow.'

237

'Well, you did in a way,' said Starstrider. 'We needed something fairly sizable to fit a cow into, just perhaps not something quite as big as this. I don't suppose our YouGet truck is still down there?'

'There's no sign of it,' said Calisto. 'It must have been towed away.'

'How about our police car?' asked Dewbush.

'The bullet-grey one?' asked Calisto.

'That's the one!'

'Yes, it's still there.'

'We can still rescue Daisy though, can't we?' asked Lucy. 'I mean, we can't just leave her here!'

They all stopped to think for a moment, before Oberon O'Brian, the Intergalactic Free Ranger responsible for accounts and marketing, came up with an idea.

'The only thing keeping the cow on the ground is its gravity blanket. If we could somehow take that off, then it would just float up into the air. And once it was high enough, all we'd have to do would be to lower the ramp at the back of the ship, scoop it up, and umbongo, we'd be off!'

'That's not a bad idea,' said Starstrider, 'but how are we going to get someone down there to take its gravity blanket off?'

'If there's a winch, or something,' began Oberon, 'then someone could be lowered down.'

Hearing that, they all looked around at each other,

in very much the same way as they'd done when the idea had been proposed that someone should run to the starship whilst holding their breath.

'I'll go!' volunteered Dewbush, seemingly happy to do so. 'I did abseiling during my Graduate Fast Track Police Training Programme, which is probably a bit like being lowered down on a winch.'

'Are you sure, Dewbush?' asked Capstan, who was considering volunteering himself, but to the best of his knowledge the 21st Century version of the Graduate Fast Track Police Training Programme hadn't included abseiling, unless of course he'd been off sick that day.

'It's easy, sir. And I could take a gun with me just in case the Mammary Clans give me any trouble. But I'd still need a winch though.'

'Right!' said Capstan, re-taking charge of the situation. 'C'mon everyone, let's see if we can find the Lieutenant here a winch,' and with the exception of Calisto, who was focussed on keeping the starship in position over the back garden of 82 Skylar Gardens, they all headed out of the cockpit to begin searching the ship for something that could lower Dewbush far enough for him to remove the cow's gravity blanket.

About ten minutes later they'd found one towards the back of the ship, near the ramp, which they lowered as Capstan attached the winch's hook to the front of Dewbush's trouser belt.

'Don't forget, Dewbush, you don't have any oxygen, so you're going to have to move fast!'

'I'll be alright, sir. It should only take me a few seconds to get down there.'

'OK, but as soon as you've got the cow's blanket off, give us the thumbs up and we'll winch you back on board. Understood?'

'Understood, sir.'

'Right!' but before sending his subordinate down the ramp and over the edge, he called over to Starstrider, 'What are the Mammary Clans up to?'

'They all seem to be lying flat on their faces. It must be some sort of Earth Cow worshiping ceremony, or something.'

'Do you think they have any idea that we're up here?'

'It's difficult to tell. But this ship is much quieter than the truck, so probably not.'

'OK, we'll just have to risk it,' said Capstan, and looking back at Dewbush, added, 'But if any of them start giving you trouble, like grabbing your leg, or anything, then you'll just have to...'

'Yes, I know, sir. I'll just have to shoot them.'

'No, Dewbush! I was going to say that you'll just have to fire a shot in the air. It probably wouldn't be a great idea if we were to kill one of them, not unless they started taking pot shots at you.'

'Understood, sir. If one of them grabs my leg, I'll

fire a shot off in the air as a warning, sir.'

'But not up at us, Dewbush!'

'Good point, sir. How about if I fired a shot into the ground, sir? Would that be OK?'

'That will have to do. Right. Are you ready?'

Dewbush loaded his gun.

'Ready, sir,' and with that he took a long deep breath before walking over towards the edge of the ramp.

As soon as he was there, Capstan looked at Starstrider standing beside the winch's controls, and called out, 'Lower away!'

They all watched as Dewbush began a rapid descent down towards the cow, and once he was almost on top of it, Starstrider slowed the winch down so that Dewbush didn't land on the cow's head, so making it the second one he would have killed that day.

Once Dewbush found himself hovering just above the cow, and with a circle of Mammary Clans all busily chanting, 'Oh Mimo Maalu ti a sin o!' which roughly translated meant, 'Oh Holy Cow we worship you!' Dewbush slipped the purple cloak off the cow's back and let it fall to the ground.

As soon as he'd done that, the cow began lifting up into the air, even before Starstrider had a chance to start winching Dewbush back up again, and so he ended up straddling the cow, as if he was riding a horse.

It was at that point that the Mammary Clan nearest to the cow who was wearing something like a Jewish Kippah over the top of his moulded pudding-shaped head, looked up from his position of horizontal prayer. Seeing their sacred Earth Cow begin to rise up into the air, at first he thought it must be ascending to heaven, as it had been prophesied to do. And he was just about to stand up and start offering his thanks to the Lord Cow of Milk for giving them a genuine bona fide miracle, when he saw that there was a human sitting on its back, pointing a gun at his head. So he decided that it would probably be better if he didn't stand up to start praising the Lord Cow of Milk, or anyone else for that matter, and instead to remain exactly where he was, just in case the human was simply waiting for an excuse to pull the trigger.

With Dewbush and the cow now clear of the ground, Dewbush decided to grip the animal as best he could between his legs, and being careful not to take hold of its oxygen mask, like he'd done the last time he was that close to one, instead he grabbed hold of some of the cow's skin around its neck. And feeling certain he had a good hold of it, stared up above him. There he could just about make out Capstan, Lucy, Starstrider and the others, all watching him, and gave them the thumbs up.

Seeing the signal, Starstrider started to winch him back up as fast as the electric motor would allow, and it wasn't long before they had both Dewbush and the cow safely on board, with Dewbush still astride it, looking very much like an apprentice space cowboy who'd thought that being one meant that they rode the cows and herded up the horses, not the other way round.

As Lucy and Oberon secured the cow to the deck so that it wouldn't float off, Dewbush climbed down off its back, saying, 'That was fun, sir!'

'That's as may be, Dewbush,' began Capstan, who was now staring out the back of the still open starship, 'but it looks like we've got company!'

Hearing that, they all looked back to see what at first glance seemed to be nothing more than an approaching storm cloud; but they all soon realised that it was no storm cloud, but more like the entire fleet of Mammary Clans' intergalactic warships, and they were heading their way.

'Get the ramp up!' commanded Capstan. 'Tie that cow down, and tell that pilot guy to get us out of here, *and fast!*'

After punching the button to lift the ramp, Starstrider took off, sprinting towards the front of the ship, closely followed by Lucy, Oberon, Dewbush and finally Capstan.

Calisto must have seen what was approaching in his side view mirrors, as the giant sized pink starship had already begun drifting upwards, steadily gaining speed as it did.

By the time Capstan had reached the cockpit, they were already shifting at quite a pace, and between breaths he asked, 'Are we going to make it?'

'I think it depends on how quickly this thing can get up to light speed,' replied Calisto, as he manually entered the word "Earth" into the GPS destination field. 'If it's anything like the YouGet truck, we'll probably be here all day!'

As the ship's GPS announced, 'Re *ipa ti wa ni iṣiro,*' which they assumed to be, '*Your route is being calculated,*' in Titanese, Capstan said, 'Well, for all our sakes, let's hope not!'

The moment the GPS said, 'Ni 500 meta, tan otun!' as it flashed up a green arrow, indicating that they should turn right in 500 yards, Calisto brought the ship around to starboard, continuing to build speed as he did, before he levelled it out and announced, 'Right, here goes nothing!' He then took hold of a large lever on the control panel directly in front of him, and saying, 'Hold on to your hats!' pushed it all the way forward.

CHAPTER THIRTY THREE

THERE WAS LITTLE doubt in Calisto's mind that the Supreme High Councillor of Titan's starship was by far the fastest thing he'd ever piloted, concluding that in space at least, size really does matter if for no other reason than a really big engine weighs nothing at all, increasing its power to weight ratio by a considerable amount. Calisto had no idea what that amount would be. All he knew was that once he'd fully opened the throttle, the starship had only taken fifty-nine seconds to reach light speed. That meant it had done 0 to 671 million miles in just under a minute, which wasn't bad by anyone's standards.

Fortunately, for himself and his crew, they were traveling in space, because had he'd tried going that fast on earth the G-force would have turned them into self-adhesive wallpaper before anyone on board had the chance to say, 'I really don't think going that fast is a great idea. Honestly, I don't.'

The starship proved equally good at slowing down as well, bringing them alongside Earth's moon at a speed where they could actually see it within only a minute of having applied the brakes, or to be more accurate, after having turned on the reverse thrusters.

And so the whole 87 million mile journey from

Titan to Earth had only taken them 52 minutes, which was hardly enough time for anyone on board to have the chance to ask if they were nearly there yet. However, anticipating that someone would no doubt be about to, Calisto called back, 'We're nearly there!'

'Already?' asked Starstrider, who was sitting on the floor with the others as they'd passed the time playing Intergalactic UNO which Oberon had brought with him.

'Quick, wasn't it!' said Calisto.

'Blimey,' continued Starstrider, getting to his feet. 'This thing must really shift!'

'I've calculated that it does 0 to 671 million miles in just under a minute.'

'Now that is impressive!' said Starstrider, as he watched Earth's moon pass them to port. 'But I wouldn't try going that fast on Earth. We'd be toast!'

'We'd be more like wallpaper than toast,' suggested Calisto.

'You're probably right.'

'Anyway, that was the fast part. Unfortunately, we've now got to get through customs.'

'Customs?' asked Capstan, who by now had stood up to stretch his legs and have a look around.

'That's correct, sir,' said Dewbush, standing up beside him to do the same. 'Any space vehicle travelling from another planet has to go through customs.'

'But we didn't have to when we went to Titan.'

'No, sir. They don't have customs there. They probably don't need it. It's nowhere near as popular a destination as Earth is, sir.'

Interrupting them, Calisto said, 'It looks like there's quite a queue, I'm afraid,' as he gazed ahead, prompting Capstan to come to the front of the cockpit to take a look for himself. He'd seen loads of queues on Earth before, obviously, but had never seen one in space, and it was something he was struggling to imagine. But nothing he could have pictured inside his head would have lived up to what he actually saw. For a start, there wasn't just one queue, but there were at least twenty of them, and each one must have consisted of at least a hundred spaceships, all of different shapes, colours and sizes.

'My God!' he exclaimed, as Calisto skilfully manoeuvred them into position at the end of what he thought was the shortest one. 'We're going to be stuck here for hours!'

'It's not as bad as it looks,' said Calisto. 'Most of these will have nothing to declare and will simply be waved straight through. However, it may be a little more complicated for us,' he added, and reached inside his gravity coat to pull out a folded piece of A4 paper, which he held up, saying, 'Can someone fill this in for me, please?'

Taking it from him, Capstan asked, 'What is it?'

247

'It's a UKA Customs Declaration form.'

Staring down at it, Capstan asked, 'Do you really have to fill all this out every time you go to Earth?'

'Only if you've been to another planet,' said Calisto. 'If you've only been to the moon, or were on a sightseeing trip around Earth, then you don't have to.'

'What about Titan's fleet of warships?' asked Capstan.

'They'll be hours yet, and I'm not even sure they'll bother coming all this way. I mean, all we did was murder a cow and take another.'

'They forced us into admitting that we'd attempted to assassinate their leader. And don't forget we stole a starship as well which apparently belongs to the guy who we were supposed to have tried to kill.'

'Oh yes. I must admit that I had forgotten about all that,' said Calisto. 'However, strictly speaking, we didn't steal the starship, as we haven't sold it to anyone, and I've no intention of keeping it for myself. It's just far too big, and I can't imagine how much it would cost to fill up!'

'That's as maybe,' said Capstan, keen not to have a repeat discussion about the legal definition of theft, 'but you're still going to have to explain that to the guy who thought it important enough to send what looked like his entire fleet of warships after us.'

'Unfortunately I can't wave a magic wand to get us through customs,' said Calisto. 'Borrowing someone else's starship is one thing, but entering Earth's atmosphere illegally is most definitely another! I'm sorry, but we'll just have to be patient and sit here for a while.'

'Are you sure about that?' asked Capstan, as he stared into the side view mirror.

'Yes, why?' asked Calisto.

But he was soon able to answer that question for himself as he too glanced in the mirror.

'Ah!' he said, moments later, having just seen what Capstan had: what looked very much like the same fleet of intergalactic warships that had been chasing them back on Titan, and which were currently dropping out of light speed en masse, and lining themselves up like an army of Roman soldiers spreading themselves out over a field at midnight.

'I'm jumping to the front of the queue,' said Calisto, with pragmatic decisiveness. 'But someone's still going to have to fill out that custom's declaration form.'

'Sod the form!' said Capstan, and turning to Dewbush, asked, 'Can't we call for backup?'

'Backup, sir?'

'Yes, you know, a large number of space police personnel dressed in full riot gear and standing behind a few hundred floating armoured cars.'

'Well, yes, sir, we could, but it would take them ages to get here, and besides, we're just the police, sir. I suspect we'd need something more like Earth's entire space fleet to fend off Titan's forces.'

'Then how can we get hold of Earth's space fleet to let them know that there's an alien fleet on the horizon?'

'I've no idea, sir, but however we tried, I suspect we'd need to get through customs first.'

By then, Calisto had used the ship's massive size to barge his way to the front of the queue, which probably had everyone leaning on their horns in protest. But if they were, nobody heard them, being that they were in space, where soundwaves can't travel, and not queuing up to get through the Dartford tunnel at the start of a Bank Holiday weekend.

'Excuse me, but you do know there's a queue, don't you?' came the voice of a beige-skinned man sitting in a small square cubicle in stationary orbit over to their right, wearing a dark blue uniform and speaking to them over the ship's intercom.

'Sorry about that,' began Calisto. 'It's just that we're in a bit of a hurry.'

'Look mate, everyone's in a bit of a hurry, so I suggest you get to the back of the line or I'll have to fine you for queue jumping!'

'Right,' said Calisto. 'And how much would that be?'

'How much would what be?'

'The fine, for queue jumping?'

'You want to pay the fine?'

'Yes, please,' he said, glancing once again into his side view mirror.

'You do know that even if you pay the fine, you'll still have to go to the back of the queue?'

'Well, that's hardly fair, is it!' Calisto protested.

'Listen, mate. What's not fair is that you've jumped to the front of the queue!'

'Yes, but as I've explained, we're in a bit of a hurry.'

'And as I've explained, I'm sure everyone's in a bit of a hurry.'

'That's as may be,' continued Calisto, 'but I'm fairly sure that they're not in as much of a hurry as we are!'

'Tell you what, mate, how about you get to the back of the line and then I can ask everyone in front of you how much of a hurry they're in. I reckon that should give me a pretty good idea if you're right or not by the time you get back to the front.'

Deciding that it was probably time for him to intervene, Capstan pulled out his Space Police ID, placed a calming hand on Calisto's shoulder and leaned forward so that the customs official sitting in the space cubicle alongside them would be able to see him. And talking into the microphone he'd seen Calisto using, he introduced himself.

'Hello officer,' he started. 'My name's Detective Inspector Capstan. I'm from the UKA Space Police.' He then turned and gestured for Dewbush to come forward. 'This, here, is my colleague, Lieutenant

251

Dewbush. We're on special space police business and need to be allowed through customs immediately.'

The customs officer peered out at them, clearly trying to see their ID's.

'Could you hold your identification a little higher, please?' he asked, clearly struggling.

Capstan and Dewbush obliged.

'It's no good,' began the custom's officer. 'My eyes aren't what they used to be. I'll have to get some new ones at some point. Hold on, let me get my binoculars,' and he ducked down out of sight.

'They're getting awfully close,' said Calisto, who'd elected to keep an eye on the fleet of Titan's warships.

Having found his binoculars, the custom's officer said, 'I've got them now,' and peered through them and read out what he could see. 'Detective Inspector Catspam and Lieutenant Dewbush, is it?'

'Close enough,' said Capstan, reminding him that he still needed to have another chat with that duty sergeant about issuing him with a replacement ID, but this time with his name spelt correctly.

'OK, I suppose I'll be able to let you through,' said the man, putting his binoculars away. 'Do you have anything to declare?' and with that he stared down at something in front of him.

'Nothing, no!' stated Capstan.

'What about that cow you've got in the back?'

Away from the microphone, Capstan asked Calisto,

'How'd he know about that?'

'They can scan the entire ship for suspicious items, like illegal aliens, cows, and suchlike.'

'And do you have licenses for all those weapons you have on board?'

'Any chance you could speed this up a little?' asked Calisto. 'They'll be in firing range at any minute!'

Doing his best, Capstan said, 'The cow belongs to Miss Butterbum,' gesturing for Lucy to step forward. There was hardly any room for her as well, so she squeezed her head in between Capstan and Dewbush, just enough for the customs officer to see her face.

'It's actually my father's cow,' she said. 'I'm just bringing it home for him.'

'And the guns?' asked the customs official.

'They're MDK 16mm Exterminators,' said Dewbush.

'And they're Space Police issue,' added Capstan, simply because he thought that made it sound more like they were theirs, and less like they'd just nicked them from an alien armoury about an hour and a half earlier.

'OK, well, that's all acceptable, I suppose,' said the customs official, and with a thin smile added, 'so if you could just scan through your UKA Customs Declaration form, making sure you've all signed and dated it, that would be great. And once you've done that, if someone could explain to me what you're doing in an intergalactic starship that's registered to a certain Lord Von Splotitty, who it says here is the Supreme High Councillor of Titan and Commander in Chief of the Mammary Clans, I'll be able to let you straight through.'

'I'm sorry, but we really don't have time to go into all that,' said Capstan.

'Then you won't be going through customs then, will you?'

Capstan sighed. 'May I ask for your name and rank?' he asked, a moment later.

'Certainly. My name's Corstick, and I'm a Senior Intergalactic Preventive Officer for the UKA Customs and Excise.'

'OK,' began Capstan. 'I'm a Detective Inspector for the UKA Space Police, so I'm pulling rank on you,' and turning to Calisto, he said, 'Take us through!'

Calisto didn't wait a moment longer, and eased forward on the ship's throttle control.

Inside his little cubicle, the Senior Intergalactic Preventive Officer surged to his feet, shouting, '*YOU CAN'T DO THAT!*'

But nobody on board the giant pink starship bothered to answer. Instead, Dewbush and Lucy simply waved goodbye to him through the window as they inched their way forward towards Earth, quickly gaining speed as they did.

CHAPTER THIRTY FOUR

'IS THERE ANY sign of them?' asked Lord Von Splotitty, who, as his intergalactic starship had been stolen, had been forced to take his family space recreational vehicle. It was a SpaceCatcher Intergalactic 9000 with a twin-turbo prop super-cooled liquid hydrogen engine that could do 0 to 671 million miles in just 48 seconds. He didn't normally like to use it, as it didn't have a bar and a Jacuzzi, and he couldn't even drive it, but it was at least faster than his starship, and could just about keep up with the MDK Time Warp SuperJet 5000s, which was what his Star Fleet consisted of, all one thousand, four hundred and fifty nine of them. It also had just about enough room for his Head of Communications, General Oblama, who he needed to pilot it, as well as Earth's Vice President, Samuel Pollock, who he wanted along for the ride so that he could kick him out into deep space if he didn't get his starship back.

'Surely they must be here somewhere?' he asked again, once the reverse thrusters brought them almost to a complete halt, parallel with Earth's moon, just behind the main fleet that had arrived a little ahead of them.

'I'm sorry, Olanla Re, but all I can see is our own

space fleet.'

'THEN GET US IN FRONT OF THEM!' shouted Splotitty, who'd lost both his patience and temper a long time before that.

'Yes, Olanla Re,' said Oblama, and began weaving his way through the hundreds upon hundreds of Time Warp SuperJet 5000s.

'And remind Field Marshal Ofeefee that if anyone puts a hole in my starship they'll have me to answer to!'

'Right away, Olanla Re.'

'And get me President Müller on the phone!'

'Immediately, Olanla Re.'

'And I could really do with a milkshake!'

'Just as soon as I can, Olanla Re.'

'And something to eat would be appreciated! I've not had anything for hours!'

Instead of agreeing to obey that last order straight away, and with a slight edge to his voice, Oblama asked, 'May I enquire which you'd like first, Olanla Re; to be at the front of the fleet, for me to remind Field Marshal Ofeefee not to open fire on your starship, to get President Müller on the phone, to make you a milkshake, or to find you something to eat?'

Splotitty narrowed his four eyes at his General, but in fairness he did have a point.

'Take me to the front of the fleet and get President Müller on the phone. Can you at least manage those two?'

'I'm sure I can, Olanla Re. And as soon as I have, I'll remind Field Marshal Ofeefee not to open fire on your starship.'

'Is there anything I can do?' asked Pollock, standing just behind Splotitty and still keen to make sure he was considered necessary, or at least vaguely useful.

'Can you make a strawberry banana chocolate raspberry and vanilla milkshake?' asked Splotitty.

'Er…' said Pollock, cursing the day he'd decided to do Chemistry at school instead of Home Economics.

'Never mind. I may still need you when I get through to your President.'

'I'll just wait here then,' said Pollock

'I'm still hungry,' said Splotitty, 'so if you could, that would be great.'

Pollock didn't like the sound of that, but felt he had no choice but to remain where he was, being that they were in the middle of space, there was nowhere to run, and the family space recreation vehicle he found himself in had barely enough room for the three of them, let alone anywhere where he'd be able to successfully hide.

'I have President Müller on the line for you now,' said Oblama, multi-tasking as best he could.

Leaning towards a microphone sticking out from the black leather-trimmed dashboard, Splotitty called out, 'President Müller, can you hear me?'

'Loud and clear, Timmy my boy, and you've called just in time to listen to me send that video over to the Intergalactic News Federation.'

'OK, well, fair enough,' began Splotitty. 'I only called to say that I think you'd probably best just go ahead and send it.'

There was silence from the other end of the line, but this time Splotitty wasn't going to simply assume that meant President Müller was considering his next move. He was fairly certain Müller wouldn't have expected him to have said that, as it effectively forced his hand, but instead of thinking of a suitable response, Müller could just as easily have been distracted by his robot wife asking if he wanted a coffee as he'd been the last time.

But he didn't have to wait long to find out.

'Thank you, Darling, but can I have three sugars this time?' they heard him say in the background.

'Did you hear me?' asked Splotitty, still finding himself unable to believe the extraordinary flippant attitude this man seemed to have to just about everything.

'Sorry. What did you say again?'

'I said that you may as well go ahead and send that video.'

'Oh good, I was hoping you'd say that.'

Cursing the day Titan had ever decided to go out of its way to discover Earth, Splotitty added, 'But if you do, you'll leave me with no choice but to launch an all-out attack on your stupid little planet which, by the time I've finished with it, will be nothing more than an asteroid bracelet!'

Behind him, Pollock chipped in with, 'I think you meant an asteroid *belt*, Olanla Re.'

But it wasn't a good time, and Splotitty turned back and shouted, 'WILL YOU SHUT UP!'

'Sorry, Olanla Re. Of course, Olanla Re. Right away, Olanla Re,' he said, and then thought he'd better just shut up as ordered.

After baring his multiple rows of yellow teeth at him, Splotitty turned back to the microphone, and the conversation he'd been having with Earth's President.

'Are you all right there, Timmy?'

'Yes, quite all right, thank you, President Müller.'

'Are you sure, Timmy? It's just that it sounded as if you were becoming a little agitated.'

'I can assure you that I'm fine, thank you for asking. Now, where was I?'

'You were saying, Timmy, how you were going to turn Planet Earth into an asteroid bracelet, although I'm fairly sure you meant an asteroid belt, as on the whole asteroids don't wear bracelets.'

Splotitty could feel himself becoming confused, and was sorely tempted to ask Pollock what asteroids wore, belts or bracelets, but he forced himself to stay focussed on the subject at hand by saying, 'Frankly, I don't care what asteroids wear, or even why you keep calling me Timmy all the time. If you send that tape, I'm going to vaporise your stupid little planet so that you couldn't even make a necklace out of it!'

'Oh yes, that's right, but I'm certainly curious to know just exactly how you intend to vaporise our "stupid little planet"?' asked Müller.

Splotitty was silent himself for a while as he let a broad smile stretch out over his face. It was time to play his hand.

'Because, Mr President of Earth, I'm currently in orbit around your puny little planet and behind me, just about, is my entire fleet of Time Warp SuperJet 5000s, all one thousand, four hundred and fifty nine of them!'

There was another moment of silence from Müller's end of the line.

'If your wife is asking if you'd like another coffee, President Müller, then I'm going to be very tempted to open fire right now!'

'No, no. I was just asking my Chief of Staff to confirm that your fleet is indeed in orbit around my planet.'

'Well, he'll soon be confirming that what I've just told you is true. So, what's it to be? The tape and any copies you've made, or the total annihilation of Earth?'

'I must say, Lord Von Splotitty, that you're proving to be a remarkably good negotiator, and much better than I'd been expecting.'

Feeling pleased to finally be getting the respect he felt he deserved, and that Müller had even started to call him by his correct name, Splotitty's mood lifted a little.

'President Müller, all I want is that tape!'

'Yes, I'm sure you do, but I've just being doing some calculations and I reckon that even if you had a fleet of two thousand Time Warp SuperJet 5000s, it's unlikely you'd be able to destroy Earth. You might be able to put a slight dent in it, but not much more.'

'And you're willing to take that risk?' asked Splotitty, 'knowing that even if we fail to destroy your planet, billions of your fellow humans will die?'

'Um…' began Müller, clearly giving that question some deep meditative thought. 'Well, I'm currently being escorted into the White House Lower Ground Floor Bunker along with my wife, the thirty-two real ones I had before her, all my children of which there are far too many for me to count, and a certain number of key members of staff. I've also just ordered our own intergalactic starfleet to launch, which consists of over ten thousand Time Warp SuperJets, but they're the new 6000 model which is the one up from yours. So I guess I'd have to say…why not, Timmy? Go on, give it your best shot!'

'Ti o Karachi-nwa meji-legged, miliki-dojuko, eniyan bi ti awon obi ti o ti wa ni ko ni iyawo si

261

k**oo**kan miiran,' cursed Splotitty, in his native tongue.

'Sorry, I didn't quite catch that?' asked Müller.

Besides Splotitty, General Oblama was about to offer the translation of that for Earth's President's benefit, which was, 'You stupid-looking, two-legged, milky-faced person born of parents who are not married to each other,' but then thought it might only serve to exacerbate the situation if he did.

But as far as Splotitty was concerned, the conversation was over, and wrapping a tentacle around the microphone so that Müller couldn't hear him, to Oblama he said, 'Get me Field Marshal Ofeefee. We may not be able to destroy the planet but by the Lord Cow of Milk, we can at least make its inhabitants burn!'

CHAPTER THIRTY FIVE

'OK EVERYONE, do you want the good news or the bad?' asked Calisto, shortly after officially crossing the border into Earth's air space.

'Why?' asked Lucy, having only just finished waving goodbye to the customs official.

'Well, the good news is that we're through customs.'

'Yes, we know that. And the bad?'

'Titan's intergalactic space fleet are still behind us, and it looks like they're ready to fire.'

'What, at us?' asked Starstrider, beginning to regret the day he'd ever suggested setting up an anti-establishment movement to free animals from the cruel oppressive practices of modern day intensive farming.

'Actually, no,' Calisto corrected himself, as he checked his computer readout more carefully. 'It looks like they're targeting Earth!'

'Earth?' asked just about everyone, all at the same time, as they stared out at the pretty blue planet that they all considered to be their home.

'It looks like it, yes!'

'At least they're not aiming at us, I suppose,' said Oberon, in an effort to look on the bright side.

'Well, they are, and they're not,' said Calisto.

'How'd mean?' asked Lucy.

'They may be aiming at Earth, but unfortunately we're in their direct line of fire, so if Earth goes, it looks like we'll go with it.'

'Can't we just get out of here?' asked Starstrider. 'The ship's fast enough, surely?'

'We could make the jump to light speed, of course, but we'd need to get clear of either Earth, or Titan's star fleet before we did.'

'They wouldn't shoot us, though, would they?' asked Oberon. 'I mean, this is that Titan leader guy's starship, isn't it? I'd have thought he'd want it back.'

'Evidently not,' said Calisto.

A moment of silence fell over the cockpit, as everyone either attempted to think of a solution, or began to make peace with God in preparation for being introduced to him, face to face.

'How long do you think we have?' asked Capstan, although he wasn't sure why. He'd nothing planned for the rest of the day, but it felt like the right sort of thing to be asking in such a disconcerting situation.

'I've no idea,' replied Calisto. 'They all seem to be ready to fire, so I guess it just depends on when they decide to.'

'What about Daisy?' asked Lucy.

'What about Daisy?' repeated Starstrider.

'Will she die too?'

'Unless her gravity blanket has some sort of an intergalactic self-defence mechanism that will protect her from just about every single one of Titan's missiles, then I think she'll probably suffer the same fate as the rest of us, along with her entire family back at home, and humanity as a whole.

It was then that Dewbush had an idea.

'Aren't Earth cows supposed to be sacred?'

'Yes, but only on Titan,' said Starstrider. 'Why?'

'Then surely they wouldn't open fire on us if they knew we had one on board?'

'Probably not, no, but I doubt they know we have one. I'm fairly sure they were too far away to see when we were loading her on.'

'Then we need to tell them!'

'But how?'

'Can't we radio them?' continued Dewbush.

'In theory, yes, of course,' replied Calisto, 'but I don't know their frequency.'

'What about using an emergency channel?' asked Capstan.

Glancing over at him, Calisto asked, 'Which one?'

'How many are there?'

'Well, there's the Police, the Fire Brigade, the Ambulance service, or the Emergency Vehicle Breakdown and Recovery.'

'Isn't there one to call in case of the imminent destruction of Earth?'

'Not that I know of, and even if there was, I doubt if Titan's fleet would be monitoring it.'

'Then we have no choice,' said Dewbush. 'We'll have to show them that there's a cow on board.'

'Show them?' asked Starstrider.

'We'll have to open the back again,' continued Dewbush, 'and float her out into space, where they can see her.'

'You know, that's not a bad idea.'

'Right,' said Capstan. 'That's by far the best one we've had so far, so I suggest we don't waste any more time discussing it, get the ramp back down and push Daisy out. All in favour, say, "Aye".'

But by that time everyone else had made their decision and had already started to climb over themselves to get to the back of the ship to shove Daisy out, just as quickly as they possibly could.

CHAPTER THIRTY SIX

ONCE SPLOTITTY HAD given Field Marshall Ofeefee the order to target Earth, after having reminded him to speak in English for the benefit of their guest, Vice President Pollock, who was still standing behind them, he'd gone on to tell General Oblama to get them to the back of the fleet where they'd be able to watch the destruction of Earth from a safe distance.

As soon as they were nearly there he leaned in towards the microphone and asked, 'Are you ready to fire yet, Ofeefee?'

'Just about, Olanla Re,' replied the Field Marshall.

'Well, can you hurry up please? Surprisingly, I don't have all day.'

'We're just waiting to hear back from everyone to let us know that they've primed and targeted their missiles, Olanla Re.'

'And how long will that take?'

'I'm not sure, Olanla Re.'

'OK, well, how long does it normally take?'

'Normally, Olanla Re?'

'Yes, normally, Field Marshal?'

'Um, well, we don't normally line ourselves up alongside a member of the Intergalactic Planetary

Trade Union with a view to destroying it, Olanla Re.'

'But I assume you've practiced this sort of thing?'

'We train for a variety of different military scenarios, Olanla Re, but I must admit that we've never conducted one where the mission has been to destroy another planet, Olanla Re.'

'Then I suggest you add it to the list of things to practice when you get back to Titan then, hadn't you?'

'Absolutely, Olanla Re, and I've already sent a memo out to that effect.'

'That's great, but it still doesn't tell me how long it's going to take though, does it? And I believe that is of greater urgency than sending memos out, especially given the fact that the President of Earth has launched his entire fleet of Time Warp SuperJets and that he has over eight thousand more than us and they're the 6000 model, which just happens to be the one up from ours.'

'We're receiving notification from the last few ships now, Olanla Re.'

·There was a momentary pause before Splotitty asked, 'Well?'

'Er, well what, Olanla Re?'

'Are you ready yet?'

'Oh, yes, we're all set now, Olanla Re.'

'Then can you please launch your missiles?'

'Right away, Olanla Re.'

'And about time too!' said Splotitty, although not into the microphone. And as he rubbed his tentacles together he gazed out at Earth, waiting for the moment when every single missile would be fired from every single one of their Time Warp SuperJet 5000s, so that he could watch them stream out towards the planet that had been the bane of his life ever since he'd discovered it, enabling him to take great delight in seeing it turn from an annoying blue colour to hopefully more of a glowing red one.

'I should have brought my camera,' he said, a moment later.

'You can borrow mine, if you like,' offered Pollock, as he pulled out his touch-tech PalmPad. 'Would you want to take a picture, or would you prefer a video?'

'Does it do video?'

'It does, Olanla Re.'

'Then I think I'd prefer that.'

Pollock set it up to start recording before passing it over.

'Thank you, Pollock. And how do I use it?'

'It's relatively straightforward, Olanla Re. You just hold it out so that you can see Earth in the screen and then press the "Record" button.

'OK, great. This is going to be excellent. And maybe I'll be able to send it to the Intergalactic News Federation afterwards.'

'Oh, I'm sure they'd love to receive a copy, Olanla

Re,' said Pollock, who had to admit that he was in two minds about watching his home planet being destroyed. On one hand it would at least make the lifeform that may be about to become his new boss happier than he normally seemed to be, but on the other he'd lose his home, his family, and his pet dog. Furthermore, he'd also miss out on any chance he'd ever have of becoming Earth's President.

Splotitty now waited, with Pollock's touch-tech PalmPad stretched out in front of him. But Earth was still an annoying blue colour, and he couldn't see any signs of any missiles flying towards it, or anywhere else, and eventually asked Oblama, 'What's taking them so long?'

'I'm not sure,' he replied.

Giving up waiting, Splotitty called out towards the microphone, 'Field Marshal Ofeefee, are you still there?'

'I'm still here, Olanla Re.'

'Why haven't you fired your missiles?'

'Unfortunately, Olanla Re, we've run in to a slight problem that I'm currently trying to resolve.'

'And what's that, Field Marshal?'

'Well, we've found your starship, Olanla Re.'

'Great! But what's that got to do with anything?'

'It's sitting directly in our line of fire, Olanla Re.'

'Can't you shoot around it?'

270

'Unfortunately, Olanla Re, it's so big that we can barely see Earth!'

Splotitty thought for a moment, before saying, 'OK, I'm willing to sacrifice my starship for the annihilation of the human species. Please go ahead and fire!'

'Um, thank you, Olanla Re, but there's another slight problem.'

'What is it now? Let me guess, you're feeling sorry for all the human beings who are about to die?'

'Not at all, Olanla Re. It's just that there's an Earth cow being floated out of the back of your starship, and none of my men seem to be prepared to open fire, just in case they hit it, Olanla Re.'

'There's an Earth cow being floated out the back of my starship?'

'That's correct, Olanla Re.'

'And none of your men are prepared to open fire in case they hit it?'

'Correct again, Olanla Re. Unfortunately, the Earth cow is a sacred—'

'YES, I KNOW!' interrupted Splotitty.

There was a momentary pause, before Field Marshall Ofeefee asked, 'I don't suppose you have any suggestions, Olanla Re?'

'I can think of one, Field Marshal, yes!'

'Oh, great. Do you mind if I ask what it is?'

'That you order your men to open fire and if they

don't, I'll have them lined up against a wall and shot, just as soon as we get back to Titan!'

'What, all of them?'

'YES, ALL OF THEM!'

'Right then. I'll relay that to the star fleet, should I?'

'Yes, please,' said Splotitty, managing to regain his composure.

'And should I include the bit about them being lined up against a wall and shot if they don't, Olanla Re.'

'If that's what it takes to get them to fire, then yes!'

'OK. Bear with me, and I'll pass that message on.'

As the line went quiet again, Splotitty said, 'I don't believe this! What's the point of having an intergalactic space fleet if none of them are prepared to shoot an Earth cow?'

'They *are* sacred animals, Olanla Re,' said General Oblama, in their fleet's defence. He himself had been brought up to believe in the Lord Cow of Milk, and certainly wouldn't have wanted to be in a position where he was forced to shoot one.

'That's as maybe,' said Splotitty, but there must be millions of cows on Earth, and I didn't hear any objections before.'

'That's true, Olanla Re, but it's probably because they can't see the ones on Earth, but they *can* see the one floating out the back of your starship.'

'We have another slight problem, I'm afraid,' came

272

Field Marshal Ofeefee's voice, moments later.

'Whatever it is, I don't want to hear it,' said Splotitty, who'd had just about enough of having to listen to all his Field Marshal's problems.

'I'm most dreadfully sorry, Olanla Re, but I really think that you do.'

With a heavy sigh, Splotitty said, 'Go on then.'

'It's Earth's Intergalactic Star Fleet. They've just left their atmosphere and will be in firing range within an estimated time of two and a half minutes, Olanla Re.'

'Then I suggest you fire all our missiles at Earth now, Field Marshal, then turn around and get back to Titan just as quickly as you can!'

'Unfortunately, Olanla Re, we just won't have time before they open fire, and once we've fired all our missiles at Earth, we'll have nothing left to defend ourselves with.'

'I have the President of Earth on Line 2 for you, Olanla Re,' announced General Oblama, and without waiting for permission, he put him through.

'Hello, Timmy my boy! I was just calling to see if you could see my star fleet yet?'

Before answering, Splotitty took a long deep breath in a bid to remain as calm as he thought it was possible to, given the circumstances.

'It would appear that we can, President Müller, which I suppose makes you think that you have the upper arm?'

'I assume you mean the upper hand, Timmy, but yes, I'd have to say that I am feeling quietly confident about our position at the moment.'

'Then I suggest that you don't know the Mammary Clans very well.'

Wrapping his tentacle around the mic again, to General Oblama he said, 'Put me through to the Field Marshal.'

Obloma didn't like the sound of where this was going, but he did as he was told and moments later, said, 'Field Marshal Ofeefee on Line 1 for you.'

'Field Marshal, it would appear that the time has come.'

'Er, for what, Olanla Re?' asked Ofeefee, with a clear note of concern.

'For us to show these milky-faced humans just what the Mammary Clans are made of!'

'Not literally, I hope, Olanla Re?'

'OF COURSE NOT LITERALLY!'

'Sorry, Olanla Re.'

'I have new orders for you, Field Marshal. I want you to launch an all-out attack on Earth's starfleet.'

'What, now, Olanla Re?'

'No, sometime next week.'

'Er…'

'YES, NOW, YOU IDIOT!'

'I see, Olanla Re. Even though we're outnumbered by about ten to one?'

'Yes, even though we're outnumbered by about ten to one.'

'And that they have the Time Warp SuperJets 6000, when we only have the 5000 version?'

'Even though they have the Time Warp SuperJets 6000, yes.'

'Right. So, basically you're telling me to send the entire fleet of Mammary Clans to their certain deaths.'

'But I think you're forgetting, Field Marshal, that we still hold the element of surprise!'

'I beg to differ, Olanla Re, but we really don't. They can see us, just as clearly as we can see them.'

'Ah, yes. But they don't know that we're going to launch an all-out attack though, do they?'

'Er, not at the moment, no, Olanla Re, but only because they won't think we're that stupid. However, the second we lock our missiles onto them, they'll be ready to engage us with everything they've got.'

'Then that's just a risk we'll have to take then, isn't it?'

'Is it?'

'Unfortunately, Field Marshal, we have no other choice. It's either that, or I hand over Titan to Earth.'

'So, it's come to that, has it?'

'I'm afraid so, Field Marshal.'

'Right then. Well, it's been nice knowing you, Olanla Re.'

'And you, Ofeefee.'

275

'O le iya re wara nigbagbogbo ṣàn ninu re gbogbo itosona.'

'And yours, Ofeefee.'

Splotitty signalled for General Oblama to end the call.

A stunned silence fell over the cockpit of Splotitty's SpaceCatcher Intergalactic 9000, before General Oblama asked, 'I don't suppose you know if there are any guns on board? It's just that I thought that maybe we could join in with the fight.'

'None that I know of, Oblama,' said Splotitty, 'although I'm not even sure where the cup holder is,' and he rested a steadying tentacle over where his Head of Communications' shoulder may have been.

'I suppose we could take a few pictures,' Oblama said, looking down at the touch-tech PalmPad that his Commander-in-Chief still held.

Glancing around at the PalmPad's owner behind him, Splotitty asked, 'Do you mind if General Oblama takes some pictures?'

But the Vice President of Earth, Samuel Pollock, seemed to have lost the power of speech, as he stared out at the two fleets who'd now begun to approach each other, struggling to come to terms with the fact that one minute he'd been thinking that he was going to lose his home planet, but now it seemed his own life was about to end.

'I don't think he minds,' said Splotitty, handing the PalmPad to his Head of Communications.

'Thank you,' said Oblama, just as the first line of missiles flew out from their own fleet heading directly for their enemy. And as he lifted it up to take a picture, added, 'You never know, we might even win!'

But then he saw Earth's ten thousand strong star fleet launch their missiles, of which there were not only eight thousand more, but each one fragmented into a dozen smaller ones the moment they'd been fired, which obliterated every single one of the Mammary Clans' and continued on to take out half their star fleet about three seconds later.

'Or maybe not,' he added, taking another picture, wondering what his Commander-in-Chief would say if he suggested they made a run for it.

CHAPTER THIRTY SEVEN

THE MOMENT Calisto saw what looked like Earth's entire space fleet rise up from his home planet like a swarm of angry wasps late for a summer picnic he felt his spirits lift, and wasted no time in telling the others the good news. And although they didn't pull Daisy straight back in, just in case Earth lost what looked like what was going to be an epic space battle, they promised each other that they would, as soon as it had commenced, so giving them all a chance to take some pictures.

The battle itself turned out to be a spectacle to behold. Despite the fact that they couldn't hear anything, being that it took place in space, it looked great! But unfortunately, from a spectator's perspective, it was very much a one-sided affair and was subsequently over rather quickly.

So it was only about three minutes later that they found themselves watching what appeared to be the very last of the Mammary Clans' warships being destroyed. It was an odd-looking one, being that it looked more like a family recreational vehicle than it did an intergalactic warship, but it didn't seem to make any difference as to its fate. The moment it was targeted by one of Earth's clever little missiles, one that fragmented into a dozen smaller ones soon after it was launched enabling it to plummet into its target from every conceivable angle, it was nothing but a distant memory.

Once the last explosion had dissipated, and all that was left was dust, debris and the odd floating tentacle, Lucy looked around at everyone and asked, 'I don't suppose someone could give me a lift home, could they?'

Just as she asked that, a cheerful sort of tune started to ring out from Capstan's touch-tech watch as it began glowing blue, and he stared down at it, trying to work out what it meant and what he should do about it.

Sensing his dilemma, Dewbush came to his rescue.

'I think someone's trying to call you, sir,' he said, as he gently took hold of Capstan's wrist so that he could show him how to answer it. 'It looks like it's the Chief Inspector, sir. And it would appear that he's been trying for quite a while.'

'What makes you say that?' asked Capstan.

'You see that number there, sir?'

'Uh-huh.'

'That tells you how many missed calls you've had.'

'Twenty-four?'

'That's correct, sir. All from the Chief Inspector.'

Capstan stared over at Dewbush, horrified to have discovered that he'd neglected to answer a total of twenty-four calls from his new boss.

'Don't worry, sir. He won't blame you. It happens all the time when we go off-planet. It's just important to remember to check your phone as soon as you get back, sir,' he said, which reminded everyone else to do the same.

'How do I answer it?' asked Capstan, thinking that he'd better, being that missing twenty-five calls was probably worse than missing twenty four, albeit only slightly.

'Just press that green button, sir. The one on the side.'

'This one?'

'That's the one, sir, yes.'

Hoping his new boss didn't think he'd been deliberately ignoring him, Capstan pressed the button, lifted the watch a little closer to his mouth and said, 'Detective Inspector Capstan here?'

'Ah, Capstan, there you are!' came the Chief Inspector's voice, loud and clear over the watch's intercom.

'Hello, sir. Sorry I missed some of your earlier calls, it's just that we only got back from Titan about half an hour ago. Then we got stuck in customs before the Mammary Clans' intergalactic space fleet threatened to destroy us, sir.'

'Never mind all that, Capstan. Did you find Sir Percy Butterbum's daughter?'

'Ah, yes, sir. She's here with us now, sir.'

'That's good. And what about that stolen cow?'

'We managed to find that as well, sir, but as it turned out, it hadn't been stolen after all. It had simply wandered off…a bit.'

'Really?' asked Chapwick.

'That's right, sir. We found it standing in someone's back garden on Titan, sir.'

'Oh well, fair enough, I suppose. As long as it's safe and sound.'

'It's here with us as well, sir.'

'Good, good.'

There was a slight pause before Chapwick continued by asking, 'I don't suppose there was another one with it, by any chance?'

'Another cow, Sir?' asked Capstan, glancing over at Dewbush, who'd started to give Capstan a homeless puppy sort of a look.

'Yes, Capstan. One of those?' said Chapwick. 'Sir Percy called in shortly after you left to say that another had gone missing.'

'Oh, um…' replied Capstan, still looking at Dewbush. But he wasn't prepared to tell his new boss the truth, that Dewbush had accidentally killed it by pulling its oxygen mask off whilst trying to get it to follow him. After all, he thought it would be highly unlikely the Chief Inspector would ever find out what had actually happened to it, and even if he did, it would be Capstan's word against an alien species, half of which had just been annihilated after what appeared to be an attempt at destroying Earth; and with that in mind he said, 'I don't know anything about another cow, sir.'

'Oh well, never mind. You've completed your assignment, even if it did take you slightly longer than I'd hoped. Now, if you could get back here as fast as you can, I have a new case to brief you on.'

'Another one, sir?' asked Capstan, suddenly feeling rather tired.

'I'm afraid so, Capstan. A fleet of fishing trawlers has just been reported missing from the North Sea.'

'Fishing trawlers, sir?' asked Capstan. He'd heard of numerous things going missing before, like cats, dogs, husbands, and most recently the occasional cow, but never a fleet of fishing trawlers.

'That's correct, Capstan.'

'Right sir. But before we return, is it OK if we drop Lucy, I-I mean, Miss Butterbum back at the farm, sir, along with her father's cow?'

'Good idea, Capstan! I'm sure Sir Percy would appreciate that. And look, as it's nearly four o'clock, you may as well call it a day after that. But I expect to see you in my office tomorrow morning at 9am sharp. Is that understood?'

'Fully, Chief Inspector, sir.'

'Right. I'll see you then, Capstan,' and with that,

Chapwick signed off.

Capstan stared down at the watch to make sure the call had ended before looking up, first at Dewbush, and then at Lucy and the three Intergalactic Free Rangers, all of whom were beaming smiles of grateful relief back at him.

'It looks like the cow wasn't stolen after all,' he said, with a wry smile, before looking over at Dewbush. 'And it's a shame we didn't see any other missing cows.'

'It was, sir, yes,' said Dewbush, before adding, 'Thank you for that, sir. I appreciate it.'

'Let's just say you owe me one, Dewbush. Right, who wants a lift home?'

But before anyone had a chance to answer, Dewbush said, 'I'm sorry, sir, but I think we've forgotten something.'

'What's that?' asked Capstan.

'Actually, sir, we've forgotten a few things. Our police car for one, sir, but also our firearms. We left them all on Titan.'

'We did, didn't we? I must admit that I'd completely forgotten about them.'

'I think it would probably be best, sir, if we popped back to Titan to try and find them. The Chief Inspector doesn't like it when Space Police property goes missing.'

Raising his hand, Starstrider added, 'I reckon we

should also head back there, to see if we can find our delivery truck.'

Capstan glanced back at his watch.

'Do you think we'd have enough time to pop back to Titan, have a look for our guns, pick up our police car, find the delivery truck, and still be back here in time for that meeting with the Chief Inspector in the morning?'

'I should think so, sir,' said Dewbush. 'And it would mean that we'd also be able to return this starship, before someone reports it as missing.'

'Right then. I suppose we'd better make a move,' said Capstan, and took a step forward, intending to head back to the cockpit, when his left leg gave way underneath him.

Catching him before he fell over, Dewbush asked, 'Are you alright, sir?' with genuine concern.

'It's my new leg, Dewbush,' replied Capstan. Until then he'd completely forgotten that it wasn't his old one. 'It seems to have stopped working!'

'Don't worry, sir. It probably just needs re-charging.'

'Re-charging?'

'Yes, sir. Bionic limbs normally need to be charged up every few days, depending on how much you use them. The medi-bot should have given you a lead to plug it in with.'

'So that's what that's for!' Capstan exclaimed, and

reached inside his trouser pocket to pull out what looked like a USB cord.

'That's the one, sir. You'll be able to plug it in once we get back to our car.'

'I see. Well I suppose that's another good reason to go back.'

And as Capstan limped towards the front of the starship with one of his arms over Lieutenant Dewbush's shoulder, the man who was the great-great-great-great-grandson of his former Sergeant Dewbush, he couldn't help but reflect back on the past couple of days since waking up in what *had* turned out to be the 25th Century after all. Since then he'd had a new leg that was far better than his old one, even if it did need re-charging every now and again; he'd visited a dairy farm in his old town of Portsmouth, now called Port's Mouth; he'd re-joined the Police Force, although apparently he'd never left; he'd flown to Titan, gone out for lunch, done a bit of sightseeing, been arrested for cow murder, tortured for attempting to assassinate its leader, escaped, returned to Earth, got stuck in customs and narrowly avoided being blown into about a billion pieces by Titan's Intergalactic fleet of warships. Thinking back, he wasn't surprised his leg had run out of batteries, and thought that he could do with a bit of re-charging himself!

And as Dewbush helped him along he found himself already thinking about his next assignment, and how exactly an entire fleet of fishing trawlers could go missing from the North Sea. *It's hardly the Bermuda Triangle!* he thought. *Or maybe, over the last four-hundred years, it's become the new one?*

No doubt he'd find out soon enough, but meanwhile he had to get back to Titan, find their guns, get their police car back and re-charge his leg. Afterwards he'd hopefully be able to get some sleep, possibly on the way home, and preferably all before the next morning's meeting with the Chief Inspector.

Detective Inspector Capstan returns in
Space Police: The Final Fish Finger

ABOUT THE AUTHOR

BORN IN a US Navy hospital in California, David spent the first eight years of his life being transported from one country to another, before ending up in a three bedroom semi-detached house in Devon, on the South Coast of England.

David's father, a devout Navy Commander, and his Mother, a loyal Christian missionary, then decided to pack him off to an all-boys boarding school in Surrey, where they thought it would be fun for him to take up ballet. Once there, he showed a remarkable aptitude for dance and, being the only boy in the school to learn, found numerous opportunities to demonstrate the many and varied movements he'd been taught, normally whilst fending off attacks from his classroom chums who seemed unable to appreciate the skill required to turn around in circles, without falling over.

Meanwhile, his father began to push him down the more regimented path towards becoming a trained assassin, and spent the school holidays teaching him how to use an air rifle. Over the years, and with his father's expert tuition, he became a proficient marksman, managing to shoot a number of things directly in the head. His most common targets were birds but also extended to those less obvious, including his brother, sister, an uncle who popped in for tea, and several un-suspecting neighbours caught doing some gardening.

Horrified by the prospect of her youngest son spending his adult life travelling the world to indiscriminately kill people, for no particular reason, his mother intensified her efforts for him to enter the more highbrow world of the theatre by applying him to enter for the Royal Ballet. But after his twenty minute audition, during which time he jumped and twirled just as high and as fast as he possibly could, the three ballet aficionados who'd stared at him throughout with unhidden incredulity, proclaimed to his proud mother that the best and only role they could offer him would be that of, "Third Tree from the Left" during their next performance of Pinocchio, but that would involve him being cut down, with an axe, during the opening scene. Furthermore, they'd be unable to guarantee his safety as the director had decided to use a real axe instead of the normal foam rubber one, to add to the drama of an otherwise rather staid production.

A few weeks later, and unable to find any suitable life insurance, David's mother gave up her dream for him to become a famed Primo Ballerino and left him to his own devices.

And so it was, that with a sense of freedom little before known, he enrolled himself at a local college to study Chain Smoking, Under-Age Drinking, Drug

Abuse and Fornication but forgot all about his core academic subjects. Subsequently he failed his 'A' Levels and moved to live in a tent in Dorking where he picked up with his more practised skills whilst working as a Barbed Wire Fencer.

Having being able to survive the hurricane of '87, the one that took down every tree within a fifty mile radius of his tent, he felt blessed, and must have been destined for greater things, other than sleeping rough during the night and being repeatedly stabbed by hard to control pieces of metal during the day. So he talked his way onto a Business Degree Course at the University of Southampton.

After three years of intensive study and to the surprise of just about everyone, he graduated with a 2:1 and spent the next ten years working in several incomprehensibly depressing sales jobs in Central London, before setting up his own recruitment firm.

Seven highly profitable years later, during which time he married and had two children, the Credit Crunch hit, which ended that particular episode of his career.

It's at this point he decided to become a writer which is where you find him now, happily married and living in London with his young family.

When not writing he spends his time attempting to persuade his wife that she really doesn't need to buy the entire contents of Ikea, even if there is a sale on.

And when there are no items of flat-packed furniture for him to assemble he enjoys writing, base-jumping, and drawing up plans to demolish his house to build the world's largest charity shop.

www.david-blake.com

Printed in Great Britain
by Amazon

49084500R00173